4.49.

smi2/07

The National Short Story Prize 2007

The National Short Story Prize 2007

ATLANTIC BOOKS
LONDON

First published in Great Britain in 2007 by Atlantic Books,
an imprint of Grove/Atlantic Ltd.

1 2 3 4 5 6 7 8 9 10

A CIP catalogue record for this book is
available from the British Library.

ISBN 978 1 84354 664 1

Text design by Lindsay Nash
Printed in Great Britain by Clays Ltd, St Ives plc

Atlantic Books
An imprint of Grove Atlantic Ltd
Ormond House
26–27 Boswell Street
London WC1N 3JZ

Contents

Preface

In 1900, on the north coast of the Black Sea, a photograph was taken which, viewed from the perspective of current literary affairs, seems beautifully evocative of the respective fates of the novel and the story. Leo Tolstoy, craggy-visaged and shaggy-bearded, lounges on a couch next to the upright, neatly bespectacled figure of Anton Chekhov. There they are: the sage of the panoramic novel, and the master of the short story. Tolstoy had little time for Chekhov's plays, but correctly admired his stories as among the great achievements of literature. There was no sense then, in Russia, that one form superseded the other. The two pre-eminent species of prose fiction were understood to be equals.

Just over a hundred years later, in Britain at least, it is the legacy of the shaggy-haired novel we have come to privilege over that of the sharp-eyed story. Why?

Perhaps it was because 1980s postmodernist thinking spread the daft idea that storytelling was outdated. Or maybe it was just a category error. We may have assumed that novels can just as well tell us stories, and because they are longer, they must be bigger and better. In fact, as Tolstoy revealed, novels are more like canvases onto which many things can be grafted: characters, ideas, social structures, plots, discourses. The novel in the right hands may be a major art, but it is not a story. Redundant as it may sound to say so, only a story is a story.

It's the impact of a single construction that the reader can absorb in a single sitting that gives the short story its formal distinction. This is not the place for a disquisition about the many things that stories may or may not be. But contemporary science offers a neat reminder of what it is that we lose if we forget them. As neuroscience attempts to find new ways of solving the old mind–brain problem, one of the analogies it routinely hits on is the idea that the brain devises the sense of a self like a narrative structure. In this sense, a story is an imaginative form that explains or echoes or expresses something essential about who we are. 'Telling stories is probably a brain obsession,' as the philosopher-neurologist Antonio Damasio puts it. 'The brain's pervasive "aboutness" is rooted in its storytelling attitude.'

On a more functional level, the National Short Story Prize is an attempt to re-align Britain's Chekhovs with its Tolstoys, and to give back some of the privileges to the short story which it appears to have lost over the last twenty years. With Radio 4 broadcasting the shortlist of five stories contained in this anthology, and with £15,000 going to the winner, it is the largest award in the world for individual stories. (£3,000 goes to the runner-up and £500 each to the others on the shortlist.) And while the partnership behind the prize covers all the principal areas of production – broadcast, magazine and book publication – it is also administered by BookTrust in England and the Scottish Book Trust, which jointly manage the national 'story' campaign, providing information and support to writers and readers nationwide (www.theshortstory.org.uk).

This year, we were fortunate to have as our judges A. S. Byatt, Monica Ali and Mark Lawson. With them, to represent the broadcast and print partners of the prize, were Radio 4's executive fiction producer, Di Speirs, and myself, as the fiction editor of *Prospect* magazine.

In order to be eligible for entry, authors had to have a previous record of publishing fiction. It was an extraordinarily competitive arena. More than four hundred entries were read, and filtered down to a longlist of around fifty stories. The final five on the shortlist provide more than sufficient evidence to justify an ongoing revival of public and publishing interest in short fiction.

The voices, tones and styles could scarcely be more different. In this deceptively slim volume, the reader will be transported from David Almond's haunting evocation of childhood in the north of England to Jonathan Falla's subtle tracing of collateral damage in El Salvador's now half-forgotten dirty war. Julian Gough revives an entire genre of high-comic Irish writing in a single bravura tale, while Jackie Kay lives out the final dream of a Glaswegian suicide. And Hanif Kureishi dares to inhabit the consciousness of an unnoticed character – the cameraman filming a terrorist execution.

Each one is an entire self, or world, doing what only short fiction can do, reminding us what we are 'about'.

Alexander Linklater
Associate and fiction editor, *Prospect* magazine

Slog's Dad
David Almond

Spring had come. I'd been running round all day with Slog and we were starving. We were crossing the square to Myers' pork shop. Slog stopped dead in his tracks.

'What's up?' I said.

He nodded across the square.

'Look,' he said.

'Look at what?'

'It's me dad,' he whispered.

'Your dad?'

'Aye.'

I just looked at him.

'That bloke there,' he said.

'What bloke where?'

'Him on the bench. Him with the cap on. Him with the stick.'

I shielded my eyes from the sun with my hand and

tried to see. The bloke had his hands resting on the top of the stick. He had his chin resting on his hands. His hair was long and tangled and his clothes were tattered and worn, like he was poor or like he'd been on a long journey. His face was in the shadow of the brim of his cap, but you could see that he was smiling.

'Slogger, man,' I said. 'Your dad's dead.'

'I know that, Davie. But it's him. He's come back again, like he said he would. In the spring.'

He raised his arm and waved.

'Dad!' he shouted. 'Dad!'

The bloke waved back.

'See?' said Slog. 'Howay.'

He tugged my arm.

'No,' I whispered. 'No!'

And I yanked myself free and I went into Myers, and Slog ran across the square to his dad.

Slog's dad had been a binman, a skinny bloke with a creased face and a greasy flat cap. He was always puffing on a Woodbine. He hung onto the back of the bin wagon as it lurched through the estate, jumped off and on, slung the bins over his shoulder, tipped the muck into the back. He was forever singing hymns – 'Faith of Our Fathers', 'Hail Glorious Saint Patrick', stuff like that.

'Here he comes again,' my mam would say as he

bashed the bins and belted out 'Oh, Sacred Heart' at eight o'clock on a Thursday morning.

But she'd be smiling, because everybody liked Slog's dad, Joe Mickley, a daft and canny soul.

First sign of his illness was just a bit of a limp: then Slog came to school one day and said,

'Me Dad's got a black spot on his big toenail.'

'Just like *Treasure Island*, eh?' I said.

'What's it mean?' he said.

I was going to say death and doom, but I said,

'He could try asking the doctor.'

'He has asked the doctor.'

Slog looked down. I could smell his dad on him, the scent of rotten rubbish that was always on him. They lived just down the street from us, and the whole house had that smell in it, no matter how much Mrs Mickley washed and scrubbed. Slog's dad knew it. He said it was the smell of the earth. He said there'd be nowt like it in Heaven.

'The doctor said it's nowt,' Slog said. 'But he's staying in bed today, and he's going to hospital tomorrow. What's it mean, Davie?'

'How should I know?' I said.

I shrugged.

'It's just a spot, man, Slog!' I said.

Everything happened fast after that. They took the big toe off, then the foot, then the leg to halfway up the thigh. Slog said his mother reckoned his dad had caught some germs from the bins. My mother said it was all the Woodbines he puffed. Whatever it was it seemed they stopped it. They fitted a tin leg on him and sent him home. It was the end of the bins, of course.

He took to sitting on the little garden wall outside the house. Mrs Mickley often sat with him and they'd be smelling their roses and nattering and smiling and swigging tea and puffing Woodbines. He used to show off his new leg to passers-by.

'I'll get the old one back when I'm in Heaven,' he said.

If anybody asked was he looking for work, he'd laugh.

'Work? I can hardly bliddy walk.'

And he'd start in on 'Faith of Our Fathers' and everybody'd smile.

Then he got a black spot on his other big toenail, and they took him away again, and they started chopping at his other leg, and Slog said it was like living in a horror picture.

When Slog's dad came home next he spent his days parked in a wheelchair in his garden. He didn't bother with tin legs: just pyjama bottoms folded over his stumps. He was quieter. He sat day after day in the summer sun among his roses, staring out at the pebble-dashed walls and the red roofs and the empty sky. The

Woodbines dangled in his fingers, 'Sacred Heart' drifted gently from his lips. Mrs Mickley brought him cups of tea, glasses of beer, Woodbines. Once I stood with Mam at the window and watched Mrs Mickley stroke her husband's head and gently kiss his cheek.

'She's telling him he's going to get better,' said Mam.

We saw the smile growing on Joe Mickley's face.

'That's love,' said Mam. 'True love.'

Slog's dad still joked and called out to anybody passing by.

'Walk?' he'd say. 'Man, I cannot even bliddy hop.'

'They can hack your body to a hundred bits,' he'd say. 'But they cannot hack your soul.'

We saw him shrinking. Slog told me he'd heard his mother whispering about his dad's fingers coming off. He told me about Mrs Mickley lifting his dad from the chair each night, laying him down, whispering her goodnights, like he was a little bairn. Slog said that some nights when he was really scared, he got into bed beside them.

'But it just makes it worse,' he said. He cried. 'I'm bigger than me dad, Davie. I'm bigger than me bliddy dad!'

And he put his arms around me and put his head on my shoulder and cried.

'Slog, man,' I said as I tugged away. 'Howay, Slogger, man!'

One day late in August, Slog's dad caught me looking. He waved me to him. I went to him slowly. He winked.

'It's alreet,' he whispered. 'I know you divent want to come too close.'

He looked down to where his legs should be.

'They tell us if I get to Heaven I'll get them back again,' he said. 'What d'you think of that, Davie?'

I shrugged.

'Dunno, Mr Mickley,' I said.

'Do you reckon I'll be able to walk back here if I do get them back again?'

'Dunno, Mr Mickley.'

I started to back away.

'I'll walk straight out them pearly gates,' he said. He laughed. 'I'll follow the smells. There's no smells in Heaven. I'll follow the bliddy smells right back here to the lovely earth.'

He looked at me.

'What d'you think of that?' he said.

Just a week later, the garden was empty. We saw Doctor Molly going in, then Father O'Mahoney, and just as dusk was coming on, Mr Blenkinsop, the undertaker.

The week after the funeral, I was heading out of the estate for school with Slog, and he told me,

'Dad said he's coming back.'

'Slogger, man,' I said.

'His last words to me. Watch for me in the spring, he said.'

'Slogger, man. It's just cos he was…'

'What?'

I gritted my teeth.

'Dying, man!'

I didn't mean to yell at him, but the traffic was thundering past us on the bypass. I got hold of his arm and we stopped.

'Bliddy dying,' I said more softly.

'Me mam says that and all,' said Slog. 'She says we'll have to wait. But I cannot wait till I'm in Heaven, Davie. I want to see him here one more time.'

Then he stared up at the sky.

'Dad,' he whispered. 'Dad!'

I got into Myers'. Chops and sausages and bacon and black pudding and joints and pies sat in neat piles in the window. A pink pig's head with its hair scorched off and a grin on its face gazed out at the square. There was a bucket of bones for dogs and a bucket of blood on the floor. The marble counters and Billy Myers' face were gleaming.

'Aye-aye, Davie,' he said.

'Aye,' I muttered.

'Saveloy, I suppose? With everything?'

'Aye. Aye.'

I looked out over the pig's head. Slog was with the bloke, looking down at him, talking to him. I saw him lean down to touch the bloke.

'And a dip?' said Billy.

'Aye,' I said.

He plunged the sandwich into a trough of gravy.

'Bliddy lovely,' he said. 'Though I say it myself. A shilling to you, sir.'

I paid him but I couldn't go out through the door. The sandwich was hot. The gravy was dripping to my feet.

Billy laughed.

'Penny for them,' he said.

I watched Slog get onto the bench beside the bloke.

'Do you believe there's life after death?' I said.

Billy laughed.

'Now there's a question for a butcher!' he said.

A skinny old woman came in past me.

'What can I do you for, pet?' said Billy. 'See you, Davie.'

He laughed.

'Kids!' he said.

Slog looked that happy as I walked towards them. He was leaning on the bloke and the bloke was leaning back on the bench grinning at the sky. Slog made a fist and face of joy when he saw me.

'It's Dad, Davie!' he said. 'See? I told you.'

I stood in front of them.

'You remember Davie, Dad,' said Slog.

The bloke looked at me. He looked nothing like the Joe Mickley I used to know. His face was filthy but it was smooth and his eyes were shining bright.

'Course I do,' he said. 'Nice to see you, son.'

Slog laughed.

'Davie's a bit scared,' he said.

'No wonder,' said the bloke. 'That looks very tasty.'

I held the sandwich out to him.

He took it, opened it and smelt it and looked at the meat and pease pudding and stuffing and mustard and gravy. He closed his eyes and smiled, then lifted it to his mouth.

'Saveloy with everything,' he said. He licked the gravy from his lips, wiped his chin with his hand. 'Bliddy lovely. You got owt to drink?'

'No,' I said.

'Ha. He has got a tongue!'

'He looks a bit different,' said Slog. 'But that's just cos he's been…'

'Transfigured,' said the bloke.

'Aye,' said Slog. 'Transfigured. Can I show him your legs, Dad?'

The bloke laughed gently. He bit his saveloy sandwich. His eyes glittered as he watched me.

'Aye,' he said. 'Gan on. Show him me legs, son.'

And Slog knelt at his feet and rolled the bloke's tattered trouser bottoms up and showed the bloke's dirty socks and dirty shins.

'See?' he whispered.

He touched the bloke's legs with his fingers.

'Aren't they lovely?' he said. 'Touch them, Davie.'

I didn't move.

'Gan on,' said the bloke. 'Touch them, Davie.'

His voice got colder.

'Do it for Slogger, Davie,' he said.

I crouched, I touched, I felt the hair and the skin and the bones and muscles underneath. I recoiled, I stood up again.

'It's true, see?' said Slog. 'He got them back in Heaven.'

'What d'you think of that, then, Davie?' said the bloke.

Slog smiled.

'He thinks they're bliddy lovely, Dad.'

Slog stroked the bloke's legs one more time then rolled the trousers down again.

'What's Heaven like, Dad?' said Slog.

'Hard to describe, son.'

'Please, Dad.'

'It's like bright and peaceful and there's God and the angels and all that...' The bloke looked at his sandwich. 'It's like having all the saveloy dips you ever want. With everything, every time.'

'It must be great.'

'Oh, aye, son. It's dead canny.'

'Are you coming to see Mam, Dad?' he said.

The bloke pursed his lips and sucked in air and gazed into the sky.

'Dunno. Dunno if I've got the time, son.'

Slog's face fell.

The bloke reached out and stroked Slog's cheek.

'This is very special,' he said. 'Very rare. They let it happen cos you're a very rare and special lad.'

He looked into the sky and talked into the sky.

'How much longer have I got?' he said, then he nodded. 'Aye. OK. OK.'

He shrugged and looked back at Slog.

'No,' he said. 'Time's pressing. I cannot do it, son.'

There were tears in Slog's eyes.

'She misses you that much, Dad,' he said.

'Aye. I know.' The bloke looked into the sky again. 'How much longer?' he said.

He took Slog in his arms.

'Come here,' he whispered.

I watched them hold each other tight.

'You can tell her about me,' said the bloke. 'You can tell her I love and miss her and all.' He looked at me over Slog's shoulder. 'And so can Davie, your best mate. Can't you, Davie? Can't you?'

'Aye,' I muttered.

Then the bloke stood up. Slog still clung to him.

'Can I come with you, Dad?' he said.

The bloke smiled.

'You know you can't, son.'

'What did you do?' I said.

'Eh?' said the bloke.

'What job did you do?'

The bloke looked at me, dead cold.

'I was a binman, Davie,' he said. 'I used to stink but I didn't mind. And I followed the stink to get me here.'

He cupped Slog's face in his hands.

'Isn't that right, son?'

'Aye,' said Slog.

'So what's Slog's mother called?' I said.

'Eh?'

'Your wife. What's her name?'

The bloke looked at me. He looked at Slog. He pushed the last bit of sandwich into his mouth and chewed. A sparrow hopped close to our feet, trying to get at the crumbs. The bloke licked his lips, wiped his chin, stared into the sky.

'Please, Dad,' whispered Slog.

The bloke shrugged. He gritted his teeth and sighed and looked at me so cold and at Slog so gentle.

'Slog's mother,' he said. 'My wife…' He shrugged again. 'She's called Mary.'

'Oh, Dad!' said Slog and his face was transfigured by joy. 'Oh, Dad!'

The bloke laughed.

'Ha! Bliddy ha!'

He held Slog by the shoulders.

'Now, son,' he said. 'You got to stand here and watch me go and you mustn't follow.'

'I won't, Dad,' whispered Slog.

'And you must always remember me.'

'I will, Dad.'

'And me, you and your lovely mam'll be together again one day in Heaven.'

'I know that, Dad. I love you, Dad.'

'And I love you.'

And the bloke kissed Slog, and twisted his face at me, then turned away. He started singing 'Faith of Our Fathers'. He walked across the square past Myers' pork shop, and turned down onto the High Street. We ran after him then and we looked down the High Street past the people and the cars but there was no sign of him, and there never would be again.

We stood there speechless. Billy Myers came to the doorway of the pork shop with a bucket of bones in his hand and watched us.

'That was me dad,' said Slog.

'Aye?' said Billy.

'Aye. He come back, like he said he would, in the spring.'

'That's good,' said Billy. 'Come and have a dip, son. With everything.'

The Morena
Jonathan Falla

He was old and pious and martyred by gout, and he kept the Morena in order, for there was a dissolute streak in her, while his was a guesthouse of repute. Señor Porfirio would not tolerate 'goings-on'. In particular, two years before, there had been a Scotchman, a journalist covering the civil war who had lodged with them, and this man had paid the Morena his attentions in the kitchen. The Scotchman, Señor Porfirio considered, had been hexed by the Morena's black eyes and by the tossing of her silken jet hair as she went about her work.

One afternoon Señor Porfirio, looking for his housekeeper, had come to the kitchen door and seen them: the Scotchman guiltily tucking some love-trifle into his pocket, and the Morena blushing to her soul. Señor Porfirio had sent the man away on the trumped-up excuse that his room was pre-booked, and put an end to the goings-on.

For the Morena was married. Yes, her husband had left her for another woman. Yes, her small daughter should have a father's guidance. But no, she was not free. Marriage is in the eyes of God, and Señor Porfirio would remark to gentlemen of his acquaintance that Archbishop Rivera y Damas would not be dissolving this one in a hurry. The gentlemen, knowing how much the Archbishop charged for that convenience, could only agree.

So Señor Porfirio, the Morena and little Chumy lived quietly together in the centre of San Salvador, in the *Hostal Santa Águeda* which catered for foreign visitors. The *Hostal* was named for a Christian virgin about whom Señor Porfirio had read in his *Diccionario Hagiográfico*; she had been pursued by a pagan ne'er-do-well who, when she refused him, had sliced off her breasts. There was a hand-tinted picture of Águeda on the dining room wall, bearing her bosom on a serving dish.

The *Hostal* was not large: only four guest rooms. The Morena and Chumy slept in a windowless cement box off the backyard. A cramped dining room dominated the centre of the house with all other rooms leading off it; even the walls were crowded, with illustrated calendars from the town's ecclesiastical suppliers. On the sideboard below Santa Águeda stood a silver-framed portrait of Señor Porfirio's brother Raoul in military uniform; he'd been a major and, thirty-four years ago, was being chased by rebel guerrillas when his jeep had toppled off a mountain track into a gully near Teotepeque.

Señor Porfirio – never moving far because of his gout – presided over the guesthouse from the dining table, supervising arrivals and departures. Each morning after breakfast, the Morena swept crumbs and wiped splashed coffee from the plastic cloth, mopped the floor and sat her little girl on a stool by the kitchen door with a tortilla and a bowl of warm milk. Señor Porfirio took his seat and with liver-spotted hands issued receipts for the room rents from a black cashbox onto which someone had stuck a gaudy transfer of the Assumption, now rather scratched.

Business concluded, the guests would return to their rooms to complete their packing, while Señor Porfirio thrust his gouty legs further under the table and settled to the right-wing press:

La Señora X will make her first visit to Florida tomorrow. To wish her Godspeed, Señora Z held a tea-party.

Nine innocent farmers killed by terrorists.

OUR ARMED FORCES NOBLY ASSIST THESE
VILLAGERS IN REPAIRING THEIR DYNAMITED
BRIDGE. WHEN WILL MINISTERS RECOGNIZE
THEIR DUTY TO GIVE EVERYONE PROTECTION?

HAPPY BIRTHDAY TO LITTLE FRANCISCO,
THREE TODAY.

After which Señor Porfirio would exercize his slow English reading on *Newsweek* magazine.

The reason for *Hostal Santa Águeda*'s tranquility was that it was not only the Morena who had mislaid her spouse. Señor Porfirio's wife had gone on a visit to Miami in 1973 and had never returned. He maintained a fiction that she was there for her health; La Señora Z had started an unkind rumour that she had wed a wealthy Cuban. But Señor Porfirio never complained. In the still corners of his heart, he knew that he had much that he desired: a respectable home, clear and correct opinions, and (let truth be told) a not un-handsome young woman to do the housework for next to nothing.

The work was done for next to nothing because Señor Porfirio was giving the Morena a haven in this world – and, he knew, she had nowhere else to go. She was a country girl, far from her own place in the northern hills of Arcatao beyond Chalatenango. That was an especially disturbed region; *Newsweek* itself had carried a report on the bloodletting there, and home visits were not undertaken lightly. But here in town the Morena had no family either, and Señor Porfirio considered himself her guardian. As long as there were no 'goings-on', he could afford to be discreetly indulgent to both mother and child.

He would look out through the kitchen and observe the little girl playing with her doll on the back step; then his old jowls would lift into something like a fond smile. He had given the Morena to understand that, when the time came, he would make her a small loan at a preferential rate to enable her to sew a First Communion dress for Chumy. There was an illustrated Bible in the glass bookcase in the master bedroom; he had bought it long ago for the baby that his wife had miscarried. In due course, Señor Porfirio would bestow this on Chumy also.

Now the foreign guests would emerge from their rooms with their unwieldy backpacks that thumped the sideboard as they turned. They'd manoeuvre past the Morena with a condescending smile and say their farewells to Señor Porfirio who would commend them to 'go with God', and then they'd be away to Costa Rica, Honduras, America and the Wide World, *El Ancho Mundo!* The Morena, stripping beds, would watch these free and easy departures – and felt herself well trapped.

At a regular hour, daily, Señor Porfirio would go out. He had an American car half as old as himself, a Rambler, into which he would ease his substantial waistline, his walking stick and his sore legs. He employed a young relative to drive him across town to a café in one of the quieter, leafier squares.

It was an old-fashioned establishment with dark wooden fittings, an espresso machine and a grinder full of beans – though these were stale and just for show; it was Maxwell House that was served. The *padron* had a commendable policy of keeping outside the bootblacks and the silent youths selling pirate cassettes, fake Rolex watches, mangoes and pornographic magazines. Señor Porfirio applauded the efforts of the poor to turn an honest *centavo*. But he came here to smoke in peace with his gentlemen acquaintances, while some played chess and others discussed the issues of the day. (Actually it could hardly be called discussion, since the little coterie were in entire agreement as to the lamentable weakness of President Napoleon Duarte, the heroism of the armed forces, the perfidy of the 'intellectuals' at San Salvador's forty-four so-called universities, and the imminent destruction of the remnants of the guerrilla bands still huddled in the long grass on Guazapa Mountain.)

After an hour there, he would call on a lady cousin who would be waiting to pose the usual questions:

'Well, Porfirio, what of that Jezebel you shelter, that Morena? Has she been sneaking out at night?'

'Remigia, my dear, the Morena may be a simple village creature but she knows who salts her tortillas. Her home district is in turmoil; I have read about it in *Newsweek*. Were I to cast her out, where should she go?'

'Straight to the Devil, Porfirio!'

'Cousin, it moves me to see her baser instincts tussle with her craving for salvation. I provide a refuge where she has opportunity for reflection.'

The Morena, heaving sheets in and out of the stone tub, generally used Señor Porfirio's absence to reflect on Scotch washing machines. She would dry her hands and secretly make free of the guest rooms. Not that she did anything much – she only looked. She would sit at the little table and peek into the washbags, gingerly extracting the toothpaste with its familiar brand names but outlandish slogans. She would stare at the bed in which the French girl or the Dutch couple had lain, feeling her heart race a little. And she'd reach out to touch the scattered underwear. In that tiny instant of contact, she imagined that the owners of the underwear spoke to her, incomprehensible but comforting, like distant angels.

Back in the dining room a moment later, she'd have Señor Porfirio's typewriter out on the dining table to write to her confidant in Scotland – dreadfully slowly, one-fingered, struggling with the spellings:

'Carido David.'

How intimate this seemed, how strong, like a deep understanding. For it was understanding that she craved; not romance, not some pathetic fantasy of passion, but understanding – and this the tall European had surely offered. He was a man of understanding, she was sure. She had, one morning, seen David polite-ly indicate the current issue of *Newsweek* on the dining table, mentioning to Señor Porfirio that to write for that important journal was his ambition.

David had returned from his appointments one mid-morning when she was sitting at the dining table mending a tear in a bedsheet. There was that day a knot of resentment in the Morena's usually placid soul; she had run short of money after buying Chumy new shoes and had approached Señor Porfirio for an advance on her wages. The old man had agreed – but only (out of principle) at a rate of interest. Once again the Morena had felt iron shackles chafing her ankles, felt that the barbed wire and bottle glass topping the garden walls were more to keep her in than to keep burglars out. Trapped, captured, constrained! She had been on the verge of rending the old miser's threadbare sheet in fury – when David had entered the house.

He had placed his heavy camera and notebook on the table while she fetched him a coffee. Pale in skin, eyes and hair, smiling readily, he had seemed to the Morena like morning light through an open door, beyond which lay – everything! He sat opposite her and chatted easily of his writing and his travels, and in return she had spoken of Arcatao beyond Chalatenango – her home village and, that summer, the scene of some furious fighting. David had pricked up his ears, asked some questions, flipped open the jotter, noted some details. Thus had begun their understanding.

'Carido David.'

She would type, laborious but keen, with a little news of the growing Chumy and of the recent guests. She was sometimes tempted to mention Santa Águeda's breasts upon their serving dish, by way of a hint as to her own chastity, but she resisted. She would have liked to include war gossip, up-to-the-minute rumour from the Guazapa front, because this was what most interested David. Soon after their first conversation, he had journeyed to Arcatao and, with assistance from the Morena's brother-in-law Juan Carlos, had made an exceedingly perilous nighttime trip to meet certain guerrilla leaders (thank Heaven, Señor Porfirio had never got wind of it). David had been enormously grateful, had sat writing in his room all the following day. But unfortunately Juan Carlos, not long afterwards, had been caught by the army, castrated and garrotted – and the Morena's supply of war gossip had dried up. So she would conclude with a tightly reined longing, always the same:

Hoping, as ever, to meet with you again in my country.
Your friend,
Berta Cruz.

After which she would sit gazing at the salutation as though to prime and charge it with something that she could not express – her suffocation in Señor Porfirio's backyard – hoping that this might spark recognition in David's understanding heart. She hoped, she dared believe it might, though she could not be sure of the reception of her letters, for David had never answered.

The Morena would fold the new letter and look across the room at the TV cabinet that Señor Porfirio locked carefully each night. She would peer at the cold, uncommunicative wood veneer as though David was perhaps in there, in that box, even now delivering a news bulletin from *el ancho mundo* that she, of all people, could not hear. She would flip the pages of *Newsweek* that David had talked of writing for – but, while the photographs intrigued her, the language locked her out as effectively as Porfirio's keys.

Or she'd glance up at the oval mirror that hung next to Santa Águeda and above dead Major Raoul. Her face, she knew, was still handsome (though much darker than any saint's), proud but with a wrinkle of laughter, her hair the glistening black of roadmaker's pitch, her cheekbones high, not angular or coarsely *indigena* but still with a hint of the hill villages, of Arcatao. Her figure was shapely and full. She had a notion (from the adverts in *Newsweek*) that men from the North did not altogether appreciate a figure quite so full. But this was of no importance with regard to David in Scotland. She did not want his body; she only wanted his attention.

With quick movements, she would stand and put the typewriter away in the sideboard lest Señor Porfirio catch her. For she remembered the expression on the old man's face when he had come to the kitchen door behind David, and the latter had blushed and stammered as he pushed the sketch map of Arcatao into his pocket. She knew that she was compromised; one false move and she and Chumy would be on the streets.

When the Union of Cooperatives announced their forthcoming demonstration, Señor Porfirio scoffed at such childish 'goings-on'. But the chess-playing gentlemen at the café in the leafy square pointed out that, if it discomfited the dismal President Duarte, it could only be welcome. Not that they need take seriously the reforms proposed by the peasantry. Duarte, however, had an exasperating habit of telling the Americans that he had popular support; it would do no harm at all to have the opposite illustrated.

Still, a tension came over the town. Rumour chased rumour; that which was whispered at breakfast was refuted by lunch, and at the café the gentlemen became unusually heated, since each believed that he knew the latest – until he was trumped by an acquaintance.

Late one morning, even as tables were being struck with emphatic force, a sudden commotion in the square outside made them all fall silent and turn their heads as one. Beneath the tables, hands groped for sticks. A hint of panic stirred in the old veins and one or two sclerotic hearts fluttered dangerously fast.

But it was neither the army nor the guerrillas, not yet a riot. Three cars appeared, streaming balloons and with a lovely girl perched on each bonnet, a sash across her bust. It was an advertisement for a private university. Blasting their horns, the cars did two turns around the square and vanished into another street. The old gentlemen scoffed again, to cover the fright they'd betrayed.

The guerrillas weren't helping the tension. Their pathetic remnants chose this time to launch several offensives of a devious, skulking sort. They blew up one of the town's transformers, so that everyone's television and refrigerator were put at risk. By day, the air force rained munitions upon the slopes of Guazapa but inexplicably failed to stop the midnight incursions, and the newspapers began to change their tone, calling upon the heroes of the military to learn to use a bombsight. Provoked and frustrated, the heroes began losing their tempers and not a few drank to excess, notably the son of Air Force Chief Bostillo who took to the streets with a skinful one Saturday night loosing-off his pistol. He drove past a police checkpoint without stopping – and was shot dead. The newspapers reported the tragedy without entirely suppressing its ironies.

All around the Morena, opinions multiplied regarding the imminent demonstration, opinions fierce, opinions dismissive, opinions subtle and cynical:

Dare they show themselves at the palace gates?

How dare they march, unless the Church be at their head!

Their daring is misplaced, for we have World Bank assurances...

They'd not dare disrupt the centre of town?!

The Americans, I daresay, will think poorly of it.

Though one might dare hope that tourists will find it colourful and amusing.

No one asked the rank and file of the unions and cooperatives what they thought. The Morena remembered her brother-in-law Juan Carlos, discovered on a hillside outside Arcatao one morning. He'd been missing more than a week, and when he was found his head was gone entirely, the top half of his body devoured by pariah dogs and stripped so clean that his spine lay neatly exposed – but his legs had been still intact inside his heavy jeans that bulged with the gases of decomposition. The Morena had always been a little in awe of Juan Carlos, and wondered if he would have approved of this demonstration. She had never had the chance to ask him much; he had always been so far away in the villages beyond Chalatenango, and so busy with Rights – and now it was too late.

She was ignorant; she knew that. She knew only that she knew next to nothing. Her reading skills were not up to *Newsweek*. She continued with the laundry, with sweeping around the stack of magazines on the floor by the TV cabinet, and with drifting into the guest rooms to visualize the Germans and the Irish, the Canadians and the Swiss, and to hear them in her head, whispering foreign news in alien accents. But when they came in at evening, these people ignored her entirely. The young Dutch couple, with their slim bodies and egotistical moist eyes, went to their room early and shut the door with a soft click.

One afternoon Señor Porfirio brought a priest to tea, a fastidious person who wiped his fingertips on a paper serviette after each nibble of biscuit. This priest had noted the picture of Santa Águeda with her breasts upon the serving dish, had made observations on the modern decline of chastity – and moments later the Morena had seen the eyes of both the priest and Señor Porfirio swivel her way, resting upon her breasts still unaccountably fixed to her ribs. She had felt herself blushing to blackness and had a moment of rage; in her life, a chance of debauch would have been a fine thing, but her desires were not of that sort! For a second she'd had the urge to wrench the wretched Águeda from the wall and smash her against the television.

She'd fled to the kitchen yard and to mending threadbare clothes. Chumy had an old biscuit tin filled with a thousand market beads, and loved to make curlicues and patterns of these on the warm cement. Around mother and daughter rose the grey walls of the yard, with iron palings so thick with bougainvillea that the back lane was completely obscured. If a demonstration or procession had passed down this lane, they'd not have seen it.

Sitting in the yard, the Morena drafted in her mind her next letter to David in Scotland. Would she write of the promised demonstration? Would she dare? There were censors...

'*Carido David*,' she typed in her painful slow fashion, once Señor Porfirio was safely out of the way and Chumy singing on the kitchen step. She stopped, she hesitated, then began again:

> *If our news reached you sooner in your country, I am sure*
> *you would be back here very quickly, and then I would be so*
> *happy to see you. There is much excitement in our town now,*
> *for there is to be a demonstration in San Salvador. I do not*
> *know what it is about – you would know better – but there*
> *will be many poor people marching. Everyone wonders what*
> *the army will do. My uncle...*

She had been about to write that her Uncle Pablo, secretary of a farm cooperative in Arcatao beyond Chalatenango, would be marching. But she stopped short, kicking herself for her lack of caution. She stared at the two incriminating words – *My uncle* – and a small storm of confusion began in her. She was proud of Uncle Pablo who, with quiet resolve, did his best to act courageously while remaining obscure to protect his family. She by no means wished to dissociate herself from him. And yet to admit to any family link, in these days...!

She had Chumy to think of too. The words were there, however, and at the end of a paragraph that had taken her half an hour to compose and type. She tried to imagine some new and innocuous sentence beginning with 'My uncle', but could not. Then she remembered that once when Señor Porfirio was typing a letter she had seen him make a mistake and rub it out. Somewhere there was an eraser for typewriting, and she remembered that the eraser had been flat and round with a hole through the centre.

She stood up, looking about the cluttered dining room. She went to the old sideboard whose once-modern, once-white laminated surfaces were yellowing and spotted like Señor Porfirio's hands. She tugged open the drawer and stirred the muddle of string and exhausted torch batteries, foreign coins and rolls of sticky tape. But there was no sign of the round eraser – and such was the Morena's concentration on the search that her normally sharp ears did not register the faint squeal of the driveway gates opening for the Rambler's return.

She looked up from the sideboard, and her eye fell on the wooden box of the old typewriter sitting where she had dumped it on the vinyl-covered couch. The eraser would be in there.

She was passing the end of the table when she heard the front door open – and she panicked. She tried to rush to the typewriter, she attempted to push her way round the dining chairs but they scraped and juddered and tangled in her path. Frantic, she reached the sofa, wrenched open the typewriter case, seized the machine from the table with the letter still in it, crammed it into the box anyhow and pushed everything under the sofa at the very instant that Señor Porfirio entered the dining room.

What are you doing on the floor?' said the old man.

'Nothing, Señor.'

'That,' observed Señor Porfirio, 'is clearly untrue.'

'I had dropped a button, Señor.'

Her face was near purple with shame. Señor Porfirio peered at her.

'What button?'

'I was mending a blouse for my Chumy.'

'Oh? Which blouse? I don't see it here.'

'No, Señor, I… I had not begun.'

'You had begun enough to drop the button. Or had you begun something else?'

'Señor?'

'Don't play coy with me, please. I do not like goings-on with buttons – or with whatever!'

'Whichever whatever is that, Señor?' pleaded the Morena.

Señor Porfirio's eyes left her face and turned slowly around the room, narrow with suspicion. The table between them prevented him seeing the typewriter box jammed under the sofa.

'I do not need to remind you, Berta, that your position in this house is one of trust.'

'I have never betrayed that trust, Señor,' replied the Morena, fighting to keep her voice steady.

'Have you not?' Señor Porfirio studied her, his watery eyes straining to see the goings-on in her head. His glance went towards the kitchen.

'I shall take my lunch shortly,' he said, 'But before that, I must compose a complaint to the Dean of a certain university.'

The Morena, visualizing the letter still under the typewriter's roller, felt her legs shake and a faint coming on.

'Or no,' Señor Porfirio changed his mind, 'that can wait till after lunch. I shall wash first. Please lay the table.'

He took himself to the bathroom; the Morena was on hands and knees before he'd locked the door.

The day of the demonstration, the sky was smeared with a thin milky humidity. David, on such a day, had said that it felt like clingfilm over the city, but the Morena didn't know about clingfilm. She tidied and cleaned and wondered if perhaps Señor Porfirio would skip his daily outing to the café, given the possibility of trouble. But Señor Porfirio was not a man to let the hoi-polloi disrupt his ordered life. The young relative appeared at 10.45 a.m. as usual, the Rambler was polished and started. The Morena was outside the kitchen sewing (real) buttons onto a blouse when Señor Porfirio came to the doorway behind her.

'I am going out,' he said, both hands on the head of his stick.

'Yes, Señor,' she returned.

There was a moment of hesitation; the only sound was of Chumy singing to herself as she drew red trees and blue animals. Señor Porfirio studied the little girl.

'Chumy will be at school with the Fathers next year,' he remarked.

'God willing,' the mother replied; Chumy would certainly never see the same school as Little Francisco Aged Three.

'She'll need guidance in this world,' said Señor Porfirio dryly, 'not having a father of her own.'

He turned inside, tap-tapping, leaving the Morena to smart.

She heard the car depart and the gates close behind it. The Morena concluded that there was no danger, and decided to take Chumy shopping.

They walked slowly, hand in hand, and the Morena's plastic shoes (one broken strap repaired with string) shuffled and slopped along the crumbling pavement. Chumy burbled a small song, and the Morena allowed herself to imagine the markets in Scotland, how vast they were, the mountains of meat and fruit there, and what she'd be buying for David's dinner…

She stopped in the centre of the pavement and frowned at herself. Fantasizing of domestic bliss in a far country! It was not more domesticity she needed, she had no shortage of that. She craved liberty, simple liberty, to do, go, think as she chose. But as she stood on the tilting concrete slabs with her daughter clinging to her hand, and tried to imagine freedom, it seemed to consist of other countries' markets and kitchens. She visualized the wide world, but *el ancho mundo* looked like infinite variants on the square at Arcatao, or Señor Porfirio's backyard. Though she was free to think and feel anything at all, she found herself daydreaming of young Dutch couples in bed, or of cooking a man's dinner, as a million other Salvadorean women would be doing today. It was not enough – but the Morena did not know what else there was! There on the pavement, her nostrils flared, as though sucking for something more.

Chumy looked up at her, trusting, silent, but puzzled. The Morena squeezed the little girl's hand and they moved on.

She disliked the market. It bulked dismally at the street's end, constructed of the same streaked concrete as the city's prisons. No one knew or welcomed you. It was an acre of dark, hot halls with stacks of soap, tomatoes underfoot and hordes of cockroaches that scampered over your shoes. There was a corner full of live and staring chickens where the stench made you retch and the wild eyes frightened Chumy, so that business there must be done swiftly. Beyond, racks of nylon blouses, and boys with trays of cigarettes, liver-salts, shampoo and ampicillin. Chumy liked to finger the blister-packs of pills, swollen hard by the heat.

Today the market was quiet: the demonstration, of course. She wondered why she had seen nothing of the expected army presence in town; perhaps they had been told to keep their heads down. But when the Morena and Chumy on their walk home reached the permanently unfinished cathedral, they came face to face with the column of protesters – and had to scurry up the steps out of the way.

The procession came towards them: first the vociferous town unions, the electricians, the printers and hospital workers with their banners: *Peace! Wages! Facilities! Dialogue!* And another: *The University of El Salvador Refuses to Die!* Now there was noise, with cheerleaders regularly spaced and shouting steadily – *Forty thousand dead in six years: enough!* – while around them the homemade placards took up the single word: *Enough!* For an instant, an image of Juan Carlos her brother-in-law filled the Morena's mind, with his spine stripped to the bone but with his jeans still on. She salivated with nausea.

An uncanny quiet fell. Into the square came peasantry in thousands, their banners held aloft in silence.

Even the feet made no noise, for most were bare; they were people from the war zones, in washed-out shirts and straw hats. The loudest sound was that of diesel trucks forced to wait as the column passed. The battered faces were not held high, but seemed weighed down by courage. They did not openly scan the bystanders but the brown eyes roamed nonetheless, apprehensive. It was not only Santa Águeda who'd had her breasts sliced off; they are good at that sort of thing in Salvador.

Gripping Chumy's hand tightly, the Morena looked beneath the banners for Uncle Pablo but in the throng of farmers she missed him. In a thousand faces passing before her was the dullness of endless loss; she suddenly wondered if Pablo was alive now; she'd heard nothing of him for months – and Chalatenango, that was not a safe place, not since the troubles that had killed Juan Carlos.

Behind the quiet cohorts came two ambulances and a truck with drums of water. There were no soldiers in the square, and few police. It was as if the authorities had turned their backs.

The Morena led Chumy home.

Señor Porfirio was late returning, though she had his lunch ready in good time. She could not understand it – until she heard, from the distant town centre, a brief crack of gunfire – two or three shots at most. She stood in the backyard, motionless, alert, straining her ears. But nothing more came. Señor Porfirio would perhaps take refuge with his cousin Remigia. The Morena went back to work, sweeping and mopping the old tiled floor under the dining table.

Moments later, she carried her bucket out into the yard and tipped the grey-scummed water down the drain. She was just putting her hand to the tap on the wall to refill, when there came a commotion in the bougainvillea, with cream and orange petals cascading to the ground. As the Morena looked up, a figure flung itself across the hedge, all limbs, loose and wild, landing in a clumsy heap in the yard. It was a young man. He had one shoe only; his shirt was ripped right across his back so that it hung in swags from his neck. He pushed himself up and stared at the Morena. She neither spoke nor moved, but stood with mop in hand. The young man's face was drawn tight with fear, his chest heaved. His eyes shot around the yard to the door of the Morena's hot little cubbyhole that stood ajar. In an instant, he was scuttling into its darkness, his bare foot slapping on the cement.

A jeep motor snarled, with orders shouted and boots pounding, and the Morena glimpsed through the bougainvillea a rush of men who barged up the back lane and away.

Left in silence again, she looked at the door of her room that was now shut. This small change was the only evidence that the tumult of the last few seconds had in fact occurred – apart from the scattering of orange petals on the cement. There was a stiff brush leaning in the corner; she seized this and swept the flowers into a coloured smudge under the iron palings. She remembered thankfully that Chumy had curled up on the dining room sofa with a picture book and had fallen asleep there. She glanced once again towards her own bedroom door, and at that moment heard a familiar drag and squeak of the driveway gates. The Rambler had returned.

Señor Porfirio entered the dining room; he was sweating and flustered. She leaned over the sofa and shook Chumy – 'Let Señor sit!' – and her daughter tottered out into the yard, rubbing her eyes. But the old man grabbed the back of the nearest dining chair, twisted and thumped down heavily. One arthritic hand dragged a handkerchief from his pocket to mop his face, the walking stick trembling in the other hand and clattering against the table leg until he dropped it. He attempted to reach down for it, but was shaking and mumbling. The Morena got there first. She put the stick on the table by him, snatched a look out of the window – and saw Chumy push open the bedroom door and step inside. The Morena felt her heart turn to ice.

'Bring water…' breathed Señor Porfirio weakly. The Morena rushed to the Kelvinator for the cold jug, and the old man gulped and trembled, dribbled and splashed the drink. Again she looked out of the window – but outside, all was still. No screams, no Chumy fleeing.

Señor Porfirio looked up at her. His clammy, pallid jowls quivered. For an instant she thought that his heart was about to fail. She hardly dared ask what had happened, because she saw the obvious answer: Señor Porfirio had been obstructed, delayed, perhaps jostled even, by the rabble of protesters, the rabble that included the ghosts of Juan Carlos her brother-in-law and possibly of Uncle Pablo too.

'What has distressed you, Señor?' she murmured. But the old mouth worked silently, the loose lips and sagging cheeks striving to put into words an outrage that was still too much with him.

Before Señor Porfirio could speak, there came a hammering at the front door:

'Open this now!'

The shouts, as the Morena went to unlatch it, seemed oddly high-pitched. But the soldiers burst in before she had time to wonder.

Four men came straight at her, and the Morena at first backed down the hall in front of them, then backed into the bathroom while they barged past. They were led by a lieutenant who strode through the narrow hallway, brutally important in dusty boots, his revolver in his hand. In all their loudness, their tight webbing, their bulging shirts, they seemed far too big for the close passageways, confined spaces and low ceilings of this house. Their sweat-stained green caps sent the light bulb in the hallway swinging; their rifles banged and chipped the paint of the door frames. In the dining room, the soldiers confronted Señor Porfirio who still sat mopping his brow.

'We must search this house…' the lieutenant began – but was stopped by a screech.

'Silence!'

When Señor Porfirio raised his walking stick above his head and brought it smashing down upon the dining table, the Morena flinched as though a gun had been fired at her. The soldiers started also, their grip on their weapons tightening in a reflex, the man at the front backing inadvertently into those behind.

'Silence!'

The cry was so shrill and angry, she thought it must bring about all their executions. She remembered the fugitive; she visualized him, desperate, creeping under her bed in a pathetic attempt to avoid detection. She felt, in anticipation, the grimy hands of the soldiers seizing her also, their clawlike fingers bruising her upper arm as they dragged her out to throw her into the back of a truck, another tossing little Chumy… She felt her knees weaken, she felt the cold sweat running down her back.

Until she realized that Señor Porfirio had stopped the soldiers in their tracks.

'Now then, Sir…' began the lieutenant. The Morena noted that already the officer's voice had modulated somewhat. It was instantly deeper, smoother, more officer-and-gentlemanly.

But Señor Porfirio was having none of him. The old face had suddenly come alive with indignation, was ablaze with outrage.

'How dare you? How *dare* you?! All my life – *all my life!* – I have paid my taxes, voted for firm government, upheld the rule of law, the honour of the armed forces! Time and again I have contradicted my acquaintances who have doubted you, I have refused to believe stories of your behaviour which, had they been true, would have been a most terrible blot! And today, today at your roadblock, I have been obstructed, insulted, even man-handled not by miserable revolutionaries but by so-called soldiers! Do you know who I am? Do you know who *that* is? Well, do you?!'

He had raised his walking stick over the table, as though he were about to bring it down for a second, even more thunderous blow – but he steadied it and pointed across the table at the silver-framed portrait of the Major whose jeep had fallen into a gully.

'That, young man, is what I call a soldier! That is a hero, a martyr! That is the man whom it was my profoundest honour to call Brother. That, sir, is Major Raoul Azorin!'

The lieutenant's right hand holding the pistol crept back until the gun was out of sight in the lee of his hip. The officer shifted his weight onto one foot and regarded the photo of the Major, then threw quick glances across the faces of his men. They revealed nothing.

'I was not aware of the connections of the house,' said the lieutenant. Señor Porfirio tipped back his head, flared his nostrils and narrowed his eyes witheringly. The lieutenant shuffled his feet. He had in truth never heard of Major Raoul Azorin.

At this moment, out in the yard, Chumy reappeared from the bedroom clutching her doll. She skipped in through the kitchen door, took one look at the soldiers – and burst into floods of tears. The Morena swept her up and buried the child's face in her shoulder.

'See what you have done. Bravo!' snarled Señor Porfirio with his fiercest contempt.

'Señor,' the lieutenant began, uncertainly, 'in the circumstances, we shall of course take your good word. Please accept my apologies. I only ask you to understand that we are searching for a dangerous young man. I… yes.'

He could think of nothing more to say. The lieutenant turned on his heel, twitched a peremptory index finger at his troops, and with a scraping of heels and a final smacking of firearms on the paintwork, the soldiers departed almost as suddenly as they had appeared.

The house was silent. Señor Porfirio, his hands still trembling, folded his handkerchief and tucked it into his trouser pocket. He glanced at the Morena.

'You are aware of the importance I place upon the good name of this household.'

'I know it, Señor,' said the Morena.

'And my distaste for goings-on.'

'Señor.'

Another moment of silence, of suspense, in which the Morena heard in the streets a last shouted order. With his hands on the table, Señor Porfirio began to crank himself into a standing position. The Morena put out a hand to assist, but he brushed her aside.

'I am not entirely decrepit, girl!'

There was confusion as his stick tangled with the chair and table. Then Señor Porfirio lurched away into his room and shut the door.

The Morena sat down, her legs all weak.

As the day faded, nor sound nor stir came from the small chamber across the yard. The Morena contrived to keep Chumy away; fortunately the evening was mild and the little girl anxious to stay close to her mother. Señor Porfirio was very quiet. He ate his dinner, watched a Mexican soap opera on television, and retired early. The Morena put Chumy on the sofa with her zoo picture book.

As soon as it was dark, the Morena turned off the kitchen light and slipped across the yard. As she pushed open the bedroom door, she sensed a black shape standing and retreating still further into the corner behind the wardrobe. The Morena whispered:

'I must put my daughter to bed in here very soon. There is a storeroom just opposite. It's open; go in there.'

A band of light striking in from a neighbour's yard just caught the fugitive's cheek; she could see a few square inches of grimy, sweaty skin. The man nodded and murmured, 'Yes.'

He stood up straight and took a step toward her. A tiny part of the Morena instinctively edged backwards – but she held her ground. The man took her hand; she felt the chill of his cooling sweat. Wearily, he leaned forward a fraction, so that his forehead touched hers. She heard his breathing, shallow and firmly under control. He put his other hand on her shoulder. They stood, unmoving.

Thank you,' he whispered, in the accent of the northern hills.

At last the man straightened and seemed in the darkness to look directly at her. She could not quite see his shadowed eyes – but in the streak of light she glimpsed the grit adhering to his cheek. She felt dirt on his hand also, and for a moment she believed she could smell on him something that was neither fear nor city – something sweeter, like harvested maize heaped in the sun, like warm soil newly turned.

The Morena found herself shy. She dropped her gaze and went back to the house.

In the dining room, she sat by the table in a position to survey the yard. As she waited, she wondered if the young man had known Juan Carlos her brother-in-law. She wondered if one day they would find this one on a hillside, with his spine stripped and his legs decomposing. She wondered what David would have made of it all – and then realized with faint surprise that she no longer cared so greatly for his opinion. A few moments later, she saw a shape flit and disappear into the storeroom. She waited for five minutes – but nothing followed, no shouts and no cataclysm of jackboots. So she put Chumy to bed.

In the morning, the store held nothing but tools and mops. The Morena cleaned as usual, in the process knocking over the tall stack of back copies of *Newsweek*. Retrieving these, she may have held in her hand the issue that reported on the troubles in Chalatenango,

with the careless photograph that had given the death
squads the clues they needed. The text would have
meant nothing to her, possibly not even David's name
on the byline. Besides, at that moment Señor Porfirio
called, with some new demand on her attention.

The Orphan and the Mob
Julian Gough

If I had urinated immediately after breakfast, the mob
would never have burnt down the orphanage. But, as I
left the dining hall to relieve myself, the letterbox clattered. I turned in the long corridor. A single white
envelope lay on the doormat. I hesitated, and heard
through the door the muffled roar of a motorcycle
starting. With a crunching turn on the gravel drive and
a splatter of pebbles against the door, it was gone.

Odd, I thought, for the postman has a bicycle. I
walked to the large oak door, picked up the envelope,
and gazed upon it.

Jude
The Orphanage
Tipperary
Ireland

For me! On this day, of all significant days! I sniffed both sides of the smooth white envelope, in the hope of detecting a woman's perfume, or a man's cologne. It smelt, faintly, of itself.

I pondered. I was unaccustomed to letters, having never received one before, and I did not wish to use this one up in the one go. As I stood in silent thought, I could feel the orphanage coffee burning through my small dark passages. Should I open the letter before or after urinating? It was a dilemma. I wished to open it immediately. Yet a full bladder distorts judgement and is an obstacle to understanding.

As I pondered, both dilemma and letter were removed from my hands by the Master of Orphans, Brother Madrigal.

'You've no time for that now, boy,' he said. 'Organize the Honour Guard and get them out to the site. You may open your letter this evening, in my presence, after the visit.' He gazed at my letter with its handsome handwriting and thrust it up the sleeve of his cassock.

I sighed, and went to find the orphans of the Honour Guard.

I found most of the young orphans hiding under Brother Thomond in the darkness of the hay barn. 'Excuse me, sir,' I said, lifting his skirts and ushering out the protesting infants.

'He is asleep,' said a young orphan, and indeed, as I looked closer, I saw Brother Thomond was at a slight tilt. Supported from behind by a pillar, he was maintained erect only by the stiffness of his ancient joints. Straw protruded at all angles from his wild white hair.

'He said he wished to speak to you, Jude,' said another orphan. I hesitated. We were already late. I decided not to wake him, for Brother Thomond, once he had stopped, took a great deal of time to warm up and get rightly going again.

'Where is Agamemnon?' I asked.

The smallest orphan removed one thumb from his mouth and jerked it upward, to the loft.

'Agamemnon!' I called softly.

Old Agamemnon, my dearest companion and the orphanage pet, emerged slowly from the shadows of the loft and stepped, with a tread remarkably dainty for a dog of such enormous size, down the wooden ladder to the ground. He shook his great ruff of yellow hair and yawned at me loudly.

'Walkies,' I said, and he stepped to my side. We exited the hay barn into the golden light of a perfect Tipperary summer's day.

I lined up the Honour Guard and counted them by the front door, in the shadow of the south tower of the orphanage. Its yellow brick façade glowed in the morning sun. We set out.

*

From the gates of the orphanage to the site of the speeches was several strong miles. We passed through town and out the other side. The smaller orphans began to wail, afraid they would see black people, or be savaged by beasts. Agamemnon stuck closely to my rear. We walked until we ran out of road. Then we followed a track, till we ran out of track.

We hopped over a fence, crossed a field, waded a dyke, cut through a ditch, traversed scrub land, forded a river and entered Nobber Nolan's Bog. Spang plumb in the middle of Nobber Nolan's Bog, and therefore spang plumb in the middle of Tipperary, and thus Ireland, was the nation's most famous boghole, famed in song and story: the most desolate place in Ireland, and the last place God created.

I had never seen the famous boghole, for Nobber Nolan had, until his recent death and his bequest of the bog to the state, guarded it fiercely from locals and tourists alike. Many's the American was winged with birdshot over the years, attempting to make pilgrimage here. I looked about me for the hole, but it was hid from my view by an enormous car park, a concrete Interpretive Centre of imposing dimensions, and a tall, broad, wooden stage, or platform, containing politicians. Beyond car park and Interpretive Centre, an eight-lane motorway of almost excessive, straightness stretched clean to the horizon, in the direction of Dublin.

Facing the stage stood fifty thousand farmers.

We made our way through the farmers to the stage. They parted politely, many raising their hats, and seemed in high good humour. 'Tis better than the Radiohead concert at Punchestown,' said a sophisticated farmer from Cloughjordan.

Once onstage, I counted the smaller orphans. We had lost only the one, which was good going over such a quantity of rough ground. I reported our arrival to Teddy 'Noddy' Nolan, the Fianna Fáil TD for Tipperary Central, and a direct descendant of Neddy 'Nobber' Nolan. Teddy waved us to our places, high at the back of the sloping stage. The Guard of Honour lined up in front of an enormous green cloth backdrop and stood to attention, flanked by groups of seated dignitaries. I myself sat where I could unobtrusively supervise, at the end of a row. When the last of the stragglers had arrived in the crowd below us, Teddy cleared his throat. The crowd silenced as though shot. He began his speech.

'It was in this place…' he said, with a generous gesture which incorporated much of Tipperary, '…that Eamon de Valera…'

Everybody removed their hats.

'…hid heroically from the entire British army…'

Everybody scowled and put their hats back on.

'...during the War of Independence. It was in this very boghole that Eamon de Valera...'

Everybody removed their hats again.

'...had his vision: a vision of Irish maidens dancing barefoot at the crossroads, and of Irish manhood dying heroically while refusing to the last breath to buy English shoes...'

At the word English the crowd put their hats back on, though some took them off again when it turned out only to be shoes. Others then glared at them. They put the hats back on again.

'We in Tipperary have fought long and hard to get the government to make Brussels pay for this fine Interpretive Centre and its fine car park, and in Brünhilde de Valera we found the ideal minister to fight our corner. It is with great pride that I invite the great granddaughter of Eamon de Valera's cousin, the minister for beef, culture and the islands, Brünhilde de Valera, officially to reopen... Dev's Hole!'

The crowd roared and waved their hats in the air, though long experience ensured they kept a firm grip on the peak, for as all the hats were of the same design and entirely indistinguishable, it was common practice at a Fianna Fáil hat-flinging rally for the less scrupulous farmers to loft an old hat, yet pick up a new.

Brünhilde de Valera took the microphone, tapped it, and cleared her throat.

'Spit on me, Brünhilde!' cried an excitable farmer down the front. The crowd surged forward, toppling and trampling the feeble-legged, in expectation of fiery rhetoric. She began.

'Although it is European money which has paid for this fine Interpretive Centre; although it is European money which has paid for this fine new eight-lane motorway from Dublin and this car park, that has tarmacadamed Toomevara in its entirety; although it is European money which has paid for everything built west of Grafton Street in my lifetime; and although we are grateful to Europe for its largesse…'

She paused to draw a great breath. The crowd were growing restless, not having a bull's notion where she was going with all this, and distressed by the use of a foreign word.

'It is not for this I brought my hat,' said the dignitary next to me, and spat on the foot of the dignitary beside him.

'Nonetheless,' said Brünhilde de Valera, 'grateful as we are to the Europeans… we should never forget… that… they…'

The crowd's right hands began to drift, with a wonderful easy slowness, up towards the brims of their hats in anticipation of a climax.

'…are a shower of foreign bastards who would murder us in our beds given half a chance!'

A great cheer went up from the massive crowd and the air was filled with hats till they hid the face of the sun and we cheered in an eerie half-light.

The minister paused till everybody had recovered their hat and returned it to their head.

'Those foreign bastards in Brussels think they can buy us with their money! They are wrong! Wrong! Wrong! You cannot buy an Irishman's heart, an Irishman's soul, an Irishman's loyalty! Remember '98!'

There was a hesitation in the crowd, as the younger farmers tried to recall if we had won the Eurovision Song Contest in 1998.

'1798!' Brünhilde clarified.

A great cheer went up as we recalled the gallant failed rebellion of 1798. 'Was It For This That Wolfe Tone Died?' came a wisp of song from the back of the crowd.

'Remember 1803!'

We applauded Emmet's great failed rebellion of 1803. A quavering chorus came from the oldest farmers at the rear of the great crowd. 'Bold Robert Emmet, the darling of Ireland…'

'Remember 1916!'

Grown men wept as they recalled the great failed rebellion of 1916, and so many contradictory songs were started that none got rightly going.

There was a pause. All held their breath.

'Remember 1988!'

Pride so great it felt like anguish filled our hearts as we recalled the year Ireland finally stood proud among the community of nations, with our heroic victory over England in the first match in group two of the group stage of the European football championship finals. A brief chant went up from the young farmers in the mosh pit: 'Who put the ball in the English net?' Older farmers, farther back, added bass to the reply: 'Houghton! Houghton!'

I shifted uncomfortably in my seat.

'My great-grandfather's cousin did not walk out of the Dáil, start a civil war and kill Michael Collins so that foreign monkey-men could swing from our trees and rape our women!'

Excited farmers began to leap up and down roaring at the front, the younger and more nimble mounting each other's shoulders, then throwing themselves forward to surf toward the stage on a sea of hands, holding their hats on as they went.

'Never forget,' roared Brünhilde de Valera, 'that a vision of Ireland came out of Dev's Hole!'

'Dev's Hole! Dev's Hole!' roared the crowd.

By my side, Agamemnon began to howl and tried to dig a hole in the stage with his long claws.

Neglecting to empty my bladder after breakfast had been an error the awful significance of which I only now began to grasp. A good Fianna Fáil ministerial speech to a loyal audience in the heart of a Tipperary bog could go on for up to five hours. I pondered my situation. My only choice seemed to be as to precisely how I would disgrace myself in front of thousands. To rise and walk off the stage during a speech by a semi-descendant of de Valera would be tantamount to treason and would earn me a series of beatings on my way to the portable toilets. The alternative was to relieve myself into my breeches where I sat.

My waistband creaked under the terrible pressure.

With the gravest reluctance, I willed the loosening of my urethral sphincter.

Nothing happened. My subsequent efforts, over the next few minutes, to void my bladder, resulted only in the vigorous exercising of my superficial abdominal muscles. At length, I realized that there was a default setting in my subconscious which was firmly barred against public voidance, and to which my conscious mind had no access.

The pressure grew intolerable and I grew desperate. Yet, within the line of sight of fifty thousand farmers, I could not unleash the torrent.

Then, inspiration. The velvet curtain! All I needed was an instant's distraction and I could step behind the billowing green backdrop beside me, and vanish. Once hidden from sight, I could, no doubt, find an exit off the back of the stage, relieve myself in its shadow, and return unobserved to my place.

At that second a magnificent gust of nationalist rhetoric lifted every hat again aloft and in the moment of eclipse I stood, took one step sideways, and vanished behind the curtain.

I shuffled along, my face to the emerald curtain, my rear to the back wall of the stage, until the wall ceased. I turned, and I beheld, to my astonished delight, the solution to all my problems.

Hidden from stage and crowd by the vast curtain was a magnificent circular long-drop toilet of the type employed in the orphanage. But where we sat around a splintered circle of rough wooden plank, our buttocks overhanging a fetid pit, here a great golden rail encircled a pit of surpassing beauty. Its mossy walls ran down to a limpid pool into which a lone frog gently plashed.

Installed, no doubt, for the private convenience of the minister, should she be caught short during the long hours of her speech, it was the most beautiful sight I had yet seen in this world. It seemed nearly a shame to urinate into so perfect a pastoral picture, and it was almost with reluctance that I unbuttoned my breeches and allowed my manhood its release.

I aimed my member so as to inconvenience the frog as little as possible. At last my conscious made connection with my unconscious; the setting was reset. Mind and body were as one; will became action; I was unified. In that transcendent moment, I could smell the sweet pollen of the heather and the mingled colognes of a thousand bachelor farmers.

I could hear the murmur and sigh of the crowd like an ocean at my back, and Brünhilde de Valera's mighty voice bounding from rhetorical peak to rhetorical peak, ever higher. And as this moment of perfection began its slow decay into the past, and as the delicious frozen moment of anticipation deliquesced into attainment and the pent-up waters leaped forth and fell in their glorious swoon, Brünhilde de Valera's voice rang out as from Olympus.

'I hereby... officially... reopen... Dev's Hole!'

A suspicion dreadful beyond words began to dawn on me. I attempted to arrest the flow, but I may as well have attempted to block by effort of will the course of the mighty Amazon river.

Thus the great curtain parted, to reveal me urinating into Dev's Hole, into the very source of the sacred spring of Irish nationalism: the headwater, the holy well, the font of our nation.

I feel, looking back, that it would not have gone so badly against me, had I not turned at Brünhilde de Valera's shriek and hosed her with urine.

They pursued me across rough ground for some considerable time.

Agamemnon held them at the gap in the wall, as I crossed the grounds and gained the house. He had not had such vigorous exercise since running away from Fossetts' circus and hiding in our hay barn a decade before, as a pup. Undaunted, he slumped in the gap, panting at them.

Slamming the orphanage door behind me, I came upon old Brother Thomond in the long corridor, beating a small orphan in a desultory manner.

'Ah, Jude,' said Brother Thomond, on seeing me. The brown leather of his face creaked as he smiled.

'A little lower, sir, if you please,' piped the small orphan, and Brother Thomond obliged. The weakness of Brother Thomond's brittle limbs made his beatings popular with the lads, as a rest and a relief from those of the more supple and youthful Brothers.

'Yes, Jude…' he began again, 'I had something I wanted to… yes… to… yes…' He nodded his head, and was distracted by straw falling past his eyes, from his tangled hair.

I moved from foot to foot, uncomfortably aware of the shouts of the approaching mob. Agamemnon, by his roars, was now retreating heroically ahead of them as they crossed the grounds toward the front door.

'Tis the orphanage!' I heard one cry.

'Tis full of orphans!' cried another.

'From Orphania!' cried a third.

'As we guessed!' called a fourth. 'He is a foreigner!'

I had a bad feeling about this. The voices were closer. Agamemnon held the door, but no dog, however brave, can hold off a mob for ever.

'Yes!' said Brother Thomond, and fixed me with a glare. 'Very good.' He fell asleep briefly, one arm aloft above the small orphan.

The mob continued to discuss me on the far side of the door. 'You're thinking of Romania, and of the Romanian orphans. You're confusing the two,' said a level head, to my relief. I made to tiptoe past Brother Thomond and the small orphan.

'Romanian, by God!'

'He is Romanian?'

'That man said so.'

'I did not…'

'A gypsy bastard!'

'Kill the gypsy bastard!'

The voice of reason was lost in the hubbub and a rock came in through the stained-glass window above the front door. It put a hole in Jesus and it hit Brother Thomond in the back of the neck.

Brother Thomond awoke.

'Dismissed,' he said to the small orphan sternly.

'Oh but sir you hadn't finished!'

'No backchat from you, young fellow, or I shan't beat you for a week.'

The small orphan scampered away into the darkness of the long corridor. Brother Thomond sighed deeply and rubbed his neck.

'Jude, today is your eighteenth birthday, is it not?'

I nodded.

Brother Thomond sighed again. 'I have carried a secret this long time, regarding your birth. I feel it is only right to tell you now…' He fell briefly asleep.

The cries of the mob grew as they assembled, eager to enter and destroy me. The yelps and whimpers of brave Agamemnon were growing fainter. I had but little time. I poked Brother Thomond in the clavicle with a finger. He started awake. 'What? WHAT? *WHAT?*'

Though to rush Brother Thomond was usually counterproductive, circumstances dictated that I try. I shouted, the better to penetrate the fog of years. 'You were about to tell me the secret of my birth, sir.'

'Ah yes. The secret…' He hesitated. 'The secret of your birth. The secret I have held these many years… which was told to me by… by one of the… by Brother Feeny… who was one of the Cloughjordan Feenys… His mother was a Thornton…'

'If you could speed it up, sir,' I suggested, as the mob forced open the window-catch above us. Brother Thomond obliged.

'The Secret of Your Birth…'

With a last choking yelp, Agamemnon fell silent. There was a tremendous hammering on the old oak door. 'I'll just get that,' said Brother Thomond. 'I think there was a knock.'

As he reached it, the door burst open with extraordinary violence, sweeping old Brother Thomond aside with a crackling of many bones and throwing him backwards against the wall where he impaled the back of his head on a coathook. Though he continued to speak, the rattle of his last breath rendered the secret unintelligible. The mob poured in.

I ran on, into the dark of the long corridor.

I found the Master of Orphans, Brother Madrigal, in his office in the south tower, beating an orphan in a desultory manner.

'Ah, Jude,' he said. 'Went the day well?'

Wishing not to burden him with the lengthy truth, and with time in short supply, I said, 'Yes.'

He nodded approvingly.

'May I have my letter, sir?' I said.

'Yes, yes, of course.' He dismissed the small orphan, who trudged off disconsolate. Brother Madrigal turned from his desk toward the confiscation safe, then paused by the open window. 'Who are those strange men on the lawn, waving torches?'

'I do not precisely know,' I said truthfully.

He frowned.

'They followed me home,' I felt moved to explain.

'And who could blame them?' said Brother Madrigal. He smiled and tousled my hair, before moving again toward the confiscation safe, tucked into the room's rear left corner. From the lawn far below could be heard confused cries.

Unlocking the safe, he took out the letter and turned. Behind him, outside the window, I saw flames race along the dead ivy and creepers, and vanish up into the roof timbers. 'Who,' he mused, looking at the envelope, 'could be writing to you?' He started suddenly and looked up at me. 'Of course!' he said. 'Jude, it is your eighteenth birthday, is it not?'

I nodded.

He sighed, the tantalising letter now held disregarded in his right hand. 'Jude... I have carried a secret this long time, regarding your birth. It is a secret known only to Brother Thomond and myself, and it has weighed heavy on us. I feel it is only right to tell you now. The secret of your birth...' He hesitated. 'Is...' My heart clattered in its cage at this second chance. Brother Madrigal threw up his hands. 'But where are my manners? Would you like a cup of tea first? And we must have music. Ah, music.'

He pressed play on the record player that sat at the

left edge of the broad desk. The turntable bearing the orphanage single began to rotate at forty-five revolutions per minute. The tone-arm lifted, swung out, and dropped onto the broad opening groove of the record. The blunt needle juddered through the scratched groove. Faintly, beneath the crackle, could be heard traces of an ancient tune.

Brother Madrigal returned to the safe and switched on the old kettle that sat atop it. Leaving my letter leaning against the kettle, he came back to his desk and sat behind it in his old leather armchair. The rising roar of the old kettle and crackle of the record player disguised the rising roar and crackle of the flames in the dry timbers of the old tower roof.

Brother Madrigal patted the side of the record player affectionately. 'The sound is so much warmer than from all these new digital dohickeys, don't you find? And of course you can tell it is a good-quality machine from the way, when the needle hops free of the surface of the record, it often falls back into the self-same groove it has just left, with neither loss nor repetition of much music. The arm…' he tapped his nose and slowly closed one eye '…is true.'

He dug out an Italia '90 cup and a USA '94 mug from his desk, and put a teabag in each.

'Milk?'

'No, thank you,' I said. The ceiling above him had

begun to bulge down in a manner alarming to me. The old leaded roof had undoubtedly begun to collapse, and I feared my second and last link to my past would be crushed along with all my hopes.

'Very wise. Milk is fattening and thickens the phlegm,' said Brother Madrigal. 'But you would like your letter, no doubt. And also… the secret of your birth.' He arose, his head almost brushing the bulge in the plaster, now yellowing from the intense heat of the blazing roof above it.

'Thirty years old, that record player,' said Brother Madrigal proudly, catching my glance at it. 'And never had to replace the needle or the record. It came with a wonderful record. I really must turn it over one of these days,' he said, lifting the gently vibrating letter from alongside the rumbling kettle whose low tones, as it neared boiling, were lost in the bellow of flame above. 'Have you any experience of turning records over, Jude?'

'No sir,' I said as he returned to the desk, my letter white against the black of his dress. Brother Madrigal extended the letter halfway across the table. I began to reach out for it. The envelope, containing perhaps the secret of my origin, brushed against my fingertips, electric with potential.

At that moment, with a crash, in a bravura finale of crackle, the record finished. The lifting mechanism

hauled the tone-arm up off the vinyl and returned it to
its rest position with a sturdy click.

'Curious,' said Brother Madrigal, absentmindedly
taking back the letter. 'It is most unusual for the crackling to continue after the record has stopped.' He stood
and moved to the record player.

The bulge in the ceiling gave a great lurch down-
ward. Brother Madrigal turned, and looked up.

'Ah! There's the problem!' he said. 'A flood! Note the
bulging ceiling! The water tank must have overflowed
in the attic and the subsequent damp is causing a crackling in the circuits of the record player. Damp,' he
touched his temple twice, 'is the great enemy of the
electrical circuit.'

He was by now required to shout on account of the
great noise of the holocaust in the roofbeams. Smoke
began entering the room.

'Do you smell smoke?' he enquired. I replied that I
did. 'The damp has caused a short circuit,' he said, and
nodded. 'Just as I suspected.' He went to the corner of
the room, where a fire axe rested in its glass-fronted
wooden case. He removed axe from case and strode to
beneath the bulge. 'Nothing for it but to pierce it and
relieve the pressure, or it'll have the roof down.' He
swung the axe up at the heart of the bulge.

A stream of molten lead from the roof poured over
Brother Madrigal. The silver river flowed over axe and

man, boiling his body while coating him in a thick sheet of still-bright lead that swiftly thickened and set as it ran down his upstretched arm, encasing his torso before solidifying in a thick base about his feet on the smoking carpet. Entirely covered, he shone under the electric light, axe aloft in his right hand, my letter smouldering and silvered in his left.

I snatched the last uncovered corner of the letter from his metal grasp, the heat-brittled triangle snapping off cleanly at the bright leaden boundary.

Snug in that little corner of envelope nestled a small triangle of yellowed paper.

My fingers tingled with dread and anticipation as they drew the scrap from its casing. Being the burnt corner of a single sheet, folded twice to form three rectangles of equal size, the scrap comprised a larger triangle of paper folded down the middle from apex to baseline, and a smaller, uncreased triangle of paper of the size and shape of its folded brother.

I regarded the small triangle.

Blank.

I turned it over.

Blank.

I unfolded and regarded the larger triangle.

Blank.

I turned it over, and read…

> gents
>
> anal
>
> cruise.

I tilted it obliquely to catch the light, the better to reread it carefully: *gents… anal… cruise.*

The secret of my origin was not entirely clear from the fragment, and the tower was beginning to collapse around me. I sighed, for I could not help but feel a certain disappointment in how my birthday had turned out. I left Brother Madrigal's office as, behind me, the floorboards gave way beneath his lead-encased mass. I looked back, to see him vanish down through successive floors of the tower.

I ran down the stairs. A breeze cooled my face as the fires above me sucked air up the stairwell, feeding the flames. Chaos was by now general and orphans and Brothers sprang from every door, laughing and exclaiming that Brother McGee had again lost control of his woodwork class.

The first members of the mob now pushed their way upstairs and, our lads not recognising the newcomers, fisticuffs ensued. I hesitated on the last landing. One member of the mob broke free of the mêlée and, seeing me, exclaimed, 'There he is, boys!' He threw his hat at me and made a leap. I leapt sideways, through the nearest door, and entered Nurse's quarters.

Nurse, the most attractive woman in the orphanage, and on whom we all had a crush, was absent, at her grandson's wedding in Borris-in-Ossary. I felt it prudent to disguise myself from the mob, and slipped into a charming blue gingham dress. Only briefly paralysed by pleasure at the scent of her perfume, I soon made my way back out through the battle, as orphans and farmers knocked lumps out of each other.

'Foreigners!' shouted the farmers at the orphans.

'Foreigners!' shouted the orphans back, for some of the farmers were from as far away as Cloughjordan, Ballylusky, Ardcrony, Lofty Bog, and even far-off South Tipperary itself, as could be told by the sophistication of the stitching on the leather patches at the elbows of their tweed jackets and the richer, darker tones, redolent of the lush grasslands of the Suir Valley, of the cowshit on their wellington boots.

'Dirty foreign bastards!'

'Fuck off back to Orphania!'

'Ardcrony ballocks!'

I saw the sophisticated farmer, who had seen Radiohead at Punchestown, hurled over the balcony and his body looted of its cigarettes by the infants.

The crowd parted to let me through, the young farmers removing their hats as I passed. The other orphans shouted, 'It is Jude in a dress!' But the sexual ambiguity of my name served me well on this occasion, as it helped the more doubtful farmers take me for an ill-favoured girl who usually wore slacks.

Escaping the crowd down the final stairs, I found myself once again in the deserted long corridor.

From far behind me came the confused sounds of the mob in fierce combat with the orphans and the Brothers of Jesus Christ Almighty. From far above me came the crack of expanding brick, a crackle of burning timber, sharp explosions of window-panes in the blazing tower. My actions had led to the destruction of the orphanage. I had brought bitter disgrace to my family, whoever they should turn out to be.

I realized with a jolt that I would have to leave the place of my greatest happiness.

Ahead, dust and smoke gushed down through the ragged hole in the ceiling through which the lead-encased body of Brother Madrigal had earlier plunged. I gazed upon him, standing proudly erect on his thick metal base, holding his axe aloft, the whole of him shining like a freshly washed baked bean tin in the light of the setting sun that shone along the corridor, through the open front door.

And by the front door, hanging from the coathook in a more alert posture than his old bones had been able to manage in life, was Brother Thomond, the golden straw bursting from the neck and sleeves of his cassock. And in the doorway itself, hanged by his neck from a rope, my old friend Agamemnon, his thick head of golden hair fluffed up into a huge ruff by the noose, his tawny fur bristling as his dead tongue rolled from between his fierce, yellow teeth.

What was left for me here, now?

With a splintering crash and a flat, rumbling, bursting impact, the entire façade of the south tower detached itself, and fell in a long roll across the lawn and down the driveway, scattering warm bricks the length of the drive.

Dislodged by the lurch of the tower, the orphanage record player fell, tumbling three stories, through the holes made by Brother Madrigal and landed rightway up by his side with a smashing of innards.

The tone-arm lurched onto the record on impact and, with a twang of elastic, the turntable began to rotate. Music sweet and pure filled the air and a sweet voice sang words I had only ever heard dimly.

'Some…

Where…

Oh…

Werther…

Aon…

Bó…'

I filled to brimming with an ineffable emotion. I felt a great… presence? No, it was an absence, an absence of? Of… I could not name it. I wished I had someone to say goodbye to, to say goodbye to me.

The record ground to a slow halt with a crunching of broken gear-teeth.

I looked around me for the last time and sighed.

'There is no place like home,' I said quietly to nobody, and walked out the door onto the warm bricks in my blue dress. The heat came up through the soles of my shoes, so that I skipped nimbly along the warm yellow bricks, till they ended.

I looked back once, to see the broken wall, the burning roof and tower.

And Agamemnon dead.

How to Get Away with Suicide
Jackie Kay

It wasn't going to be easy. For one thing, too much was known about Malcolm. He wasn't one of those sad cases that had no friends. By the time he was forty-five, he'd gathered arguably too many friends. They knew, for instance, that Malcolm was a very good driver and there was no way in the creation that he'd end up with his metal wrapped around a lamppost, or with his bonnet stuck in the birch tree at the end of his old street, or his car up-ended on the central reservation of the M8 to Edinburgh. 'Reserve your judgements on that one,' he could imagine his pals saying, softly, 'cos Malkie wis an excellent driver. All right – one drink-driving offence, but Malkie never knocked down anything. No no no no. Something's fishy; we're talking suicide here.'

The thing was, Malcolm badly wanted to kill himself: he wanted the noise to stop; he wanted the silence that pads across a loch on a wintry, misty morning with its webbed feet. No more demands, Malcolm wanted not to have to tell himself all the ways in which he hadn't really done what he thought he might do with his life. But he didn't want anybody knowing he'd killed himself. Just because he wanted to die didn't mean he'd lost his pride. That might be a contradiction for some people to think about; and some people might think that if you got that desperate you really wouldn't care what people thought. You would actually be beyond it. Well, Malcolm wasn't beyond it. He respected the living. Face it: suicide's a bum deal. He didn't want his mates feeling bad for years, thinking, Right enough, he didn't sound himself. Should have taken him for a pint. Or should have this, should have that. He didn't even want his ex-wife to feel rotten, despite the not insignificant fact that she was the one that dumped him, took his kids and got a big stupid eedyit to prance around and pretend to be their father. Try that out. If somebody's pretending to be you, Malcolm thought, then who are you? Would it be noticed really, in a significant, life-changing way? He doubted it. He had loved his wife once. He was categorically not interested in revenging her for betraying him. Malcolm would actually be the first to acknowledge that he had been a miserable bastard for years. Katie was entitled to her wee portion of happiness. 'Do you mean that, Malkie?'

'Naw; aye. I wanted to be dead, very dead indeed, more dead than a dodo.' Thinking about death was a non-stop conversation in Malcolm's head. He played the parts, as if a jury were involved. For him acquittal was being allowed to quit, to make a rapid exit, to say, Ta ta, I'm away. Will ye no come back again? No, frankly.

People say if you've got running water you are lucky; if you've got food you are lucky; if you've got drink you are lucky. If you are hanging around Glasgow Cross out of your mind, with the big black dog snapping at your heels, running water is actually not much use to you. Do you know? You find yourself… That's it; you find yourself in situations you wouldn't have put your-self in when you were a boy, staggering outside the Old Tollbooth Bar at the top of Saltmarket near the Gallowgate bawling your eyes out like a baby. Why? Who knows why about anything really. We think we know why and we don't know why and we can't cope with not knowing why; that's about all Malcolm could think to say about why.

But by the way, *why* was not what interested him. When, now that was the big juicy question. *When* could he do it and how, there was another massive word. Hoooooowwwwww. Saying how made him feel good. Howwwwwwwwww. He held on to the *wih* sound. Aye. The two big words coming into Malcolm's brain in the freezing December Glasgow cold were when and how. But not why. Why did not actually get a look in. How. When. When How. He walked up Buchanan Street, turned left into West George Street, crossed West Nile Street, crossed Renfield Street to Hope Street, walked up the top of Hope Street into Sauchiehall Street. It was chucking it down. The kind of rain that's got fucking cold fingers like your daddy's mammy or, Christ, admit it your ex-wife's. She always had cold fingers. She used to say 'cold hands, warm heart', but that turned out to be nonsense because her heart was certainly not warm. Ice is not even near the ball park. Polar fucking frosty fucking frigid freezer fucking frozen peas heart. But let's not go there. Malcolm tries not to think of Katie these days. It just brings him down and he wants to be up, up up up, enough to enjoy thinking about how he can get away with it. Come on, come on, Malkie, he says to himself, for goodness' sake, son, are you going to be able to pull this one off?

Malcolm had always been a pernickety man who enjoyed puzzles and this was the biggest one of his entire life: how to kill himself and make it look like an accident. When the black dog came for him with its frothy mouth in the winter months of his marriage, he was always kept away from just tying a rope to the garage fucking ceiling because of the offspring, because of Lucy and Jojo and the wee man. But now he is not getting to see his bairns. He says the word bairns when he is full of self-pity, because it brings him close to tears. He likes a word that makes him greet. Katie can tell all the lies she wants, but Malcolm was a good daddy to them and she fucking knows it. So there you are. He didn't just turn the box on, sit them down in front of it like zombies and dump burgers and chips, fish and chips, pie and chips and pizza and chips on the three bairns. No. He did things with them and he made soup and he didn't smoke around them. He made excellent broth, by the way. And was always on the lookout for something interesting to do with them, because Malcolm had taught himself most of what he knew and he wanted to teach them too. He took the bairns to the oldest house in Glasgow. He took them to the art galleries. Malcolm's offspring had been to every place in Glasgow that has a painting: Kelvinside Art Galleries, the Modern Art thingimigig with the different-flavoured floors, near where the old Music and Drama building was. If you've lived in Glasgow as long as Malcolm, you always remembered what build-ings used to be where. It was disconcerting, like you were living a double life, half in the dark Glasgow past, long before they ever cleaned up the sandstone.

If Malcolm was a building and he could simply clean up his sandstone, things wouldn't be all that bad. Glasgow's changed; it used to be a very dark city and now it's light. Malcolm considered being a tour guide for Glasgow and he went into the tourist board to make that very suggestion and they took his name and put it in a file. He goes to Buchanan Street bus station to get the bus back to the Milton. He is wary of driving at the moment and anyway the road tax has run out. Probably the tourist board will ring up when I've called it all off, when I'm totally dead, Malcolm thought, when the game's a bogey. What else with the bairns, then? Burrell, Christ, even the Burrell, which is a bit out of the way, and used up a lot of petrol. The redundancy money was running out fast, but better spent on art than on shite. The bairns liked that American with the dark paintings in the McClennan Galleries in Sauchiehall Street, the one whose widow left his brushes and stuff to Glasgow because she didn't want the Yanks tae have his intimate brushes, what was his name? The brain's a sieve. Soon, soon there would be no need to remember anything. Can you imagine the relief of that? Malcolm tried to imagine a time when he wouldn't have to be learning new things, when this burden that he placed on himself of trying to be cleverer than he actually was, was lifted and he was free.

Up until fairly recently, Malcolm had been enjoying listening to classical music. He listened to Radio 3, which was a whole education for him by the way, a complete education. This morning he cried his eyes out when they played Strauss, *Transformation*. It's raining now, very dreich. When it rains like that, dark in the afternoon, you feel like you've been taken into the past. If you can transform, if you can change, maybe you don't have to bump yourself off, you know. If you can transform maybe you can live – Whistler, that's the name. Good. That would have bugged him all day and taken the edge off concentrating on his plan: the total but secret destruction of Malcolm Henry Jobson. Transformation. He got to his small house, turned the key in the door. The hardest thing now about living on his own was returning home to an empty house. Putting the key in and braving it through the hall. It was so quiet in his house; the only thing that welcomed him was the dog. He fell into his bed and slept the drink off for a bit.

He thought about transformation and he looked in the bathroom mirror. Another night on the sauce. Can't even remember falling into his bed. His eyes were hanging out of their sockets, like the sockets were dodgy plugs. His face rough like a dog's arse. He is going bald. He is too wiry; he is not a pretty sight. Her going with Him has made him feel like a wee nyaff. Don't ask him how it's done this, but it's made him smaller in height. When he was married he was five foot eight, now he looks about five five at the most. The new man is a handsome big bastard. He can say that because – quite catastrophically for Malcolm – it's the truth. And he doesn't have a tattoo. Malcolm's got a fucking big stupid tattoo down his arm. A map of Scotland with Katie's name across it and a wee snake in the bottom left-hand corner in blue. She turns her nose up at the tattoo now. It's not fair encouraging your bloke to have a tattoo years ago when you loved the shape of his arse and liked a candy floss in the Kelvin Hall to turn around, years later, when you've gone all hoity-toity because you've gone to a night class and met a posh geezer from Newton Mearns, and say that tattoos are naff. It's no right. Malcolm would have had it removed but he loathes pain and there's no point now anyway. Well, maybe there is. He'll have a think. Does he want to go wherever he is going with this tattoo still on him? is question number one. And question number two is: wouldn't having this tattoo removed, painful though it very well might be, be preparation for the inevitable pain of suicide?

What does she do – the one that said she'd love him for ever – to think he used to stop her and say, 'I don't believe in the for ever bit, baby, let's live just for today'– she goes off and falls in love with the fair-haired dickhead, hair that falls over his face like a pansy, and presumably, she's told him the same bullshit now, how she's going to love him for ever. Well. She's said to him, 'Malcolm' – because she's back to calling him his official name that no one calls him – 'Malcolm, we could have done without your jealousy.' Well, he could have done without it too, you know. Then she said, 'This isn't love, this jealousy, this is just pure selfishness pretending to be love.' It's not enough that she's broken his heart, broken his home and ripped him off, taken his kids, set up with another man who is pretending to be their daddy, you know, but he is to be accused of being selfish?

The other reason Malcolm wanted to kill himself without anybody knowing that he'd committed suicide is that people who commit suicide have got a poor reputation and are accused after the event of being selfish. How about that, eh? Can you imagine anything worse? You feel that bad you want the suck of a cold gun inside your mouth and the people surrounding the people left behind mutter at your funeral, 'What a terrible thing to do, what a dreadful selfish thing to do.' I mean fucking excuse me, Malcolm thought. YOUR'RE NOT IN YOUR RIGHT MIND. Trees, flowers, butterflies, children, going to China one day maybe, or going to – where else was it that you wanted to go? Doesn't matter. Friends, your mother, money, work, daft memories, dog, house, none of it matters. All that stuff is all very silly. It's only love that matters in the end and when that goes, you don't frankly give a donkey's toss about anything, anything at all. The only beautiful thing left to you is death.

Silence, you know. Like shut the fuck up because I'm no listening to this crap any more; Malcolm was pacing his room now, talking to himself out loud. 'I don't have to do this – live.'

One of the nicest things that happened before they all split the house up was Lucy coming in from school to say that she'd got two house points: one for writing beautiful sentences and the other for writing on the line beautifully with a sharp pencil. Malcolm said to her, 'I'm proud of you, Luce,' and then he went upstairs and threw up in the toilet.

Options. They have that for the movies, don't they? Option this, option that. Option One. Get some deadly poison and take it slowly over a period of time. But the thought of constant diarrhoea and gut pains is not very pleasing. Because Malcolm is a terrible coward when it comes to pain, it is actually very difficult trying to find a solution to his problem. Most methods of suicide are painful whether they look like suicide or not. Throttling yourself must be sore and nobody really knows how long it takes once you kick the chair from under your feet. Ditto slashing your wrists and anyway you couldn't make that look like an accident. He thought of just walking out in front of a car on the bypass but then he'd be giving some total stranger a nasty raw deal; he's got that on his conscience, even if he says to himself, 'There was nothing I could do, he just stepped right out in front of me,' he'll be haunted for years and years to come. He could go up on his roof ostensibly to fix his chimney or TV aerial or something and just fall off. But he is not the kind of bloke that ever goes on his roof. Malcolm is not a handyman. He half envies and half despises handymen. DIY fuckers, fussing over this and that, making a mess actually for people when they move into your house and have to inherit spangled wiring.

Not long after Malcolm was made redundant, he discovered that she was at it with Him. That was a double blow. And he's not short of a bob or two either. You should see the stuff he's bought Malcolm's bairns. Computers and Barbies and GameBoys and Disney dressing-up clothes and DVD machines and a big karaoke machine. Apparently Jamie fancies himself as a bit of a Frank Sinatra. One night before Katie was properly with Jamie, she confessed to Malcolm that Jamie said, 'Only two people can phrase in this world, me and Frank Sinatra.' The tears poured down Malcolm's face, he was killing himself so much.

Malcolm is not into material things in any case. Never needs much to get by. He doesn't think it's good for kids to get this and then get that and then get something else. But when, in the early days (when she was still letting him see them before she took out a court order just because he took a hammer to the new computer like a Luddite), he said anything about materialism, she just raised her eyebrows and said, 'Sour grapes, Malcolm, be happy for us. The kids don't want for anything now and that's lovely for them.' He is supposed to be happy when his kids have transformed before his very eyes into spoilt brats. He is supposed to welcome this? Being in love has made his ex-wife very insensitive. Here's a wee example: 'I'm sorry, Malcolm, but now that I'm with Jamie, I really know what love is. I thought it was love with you, but it wasn't. I can't help my feelings. Every time I see him I go weak at the knees.' When she said that to Malcolm, strange music came into his head, angry octaves that he'd been listening to the day before. A piece by Schubert, if he remembers correctly. The man wasn't well when he wrote it. Poor bastard. Some of that music is no right in the head. It gets right in and starts to play itself to you even when it's not playing. He blinked, that time, and didn't say anything. On the one hand, she was hypersensitive to Jamie and everything he wanted and all his feelings. Malcolm couldn't go in when he went to pick up his kids because Jamie found it difficult. He couldn't ring after six because Jamie found it difficult. He couldn't fucking breathe because Jamie found it difficult. *It'll no be long now.* And on the other hand she didn't seem to give a horse's toss about Malcolm's feelings. She was like a woman driven, a woman possessed.

Och, enough. He loved her and she didn't love him not like he loved her and that is the story – end of story – of most people's love. There's always somebody who loves a bit more; somebody who loves a bit less. I'd be surprised if that big bastard doesn't break my wife's heart. I hope he doesn't, Malcolm thought. He was still pacing. He was a bit hungry actually, but he couldn't think of stopping for food. He couldn't exactly rush out for a last fish supper. No. He is not petty. Believe you me, he says to himself, I've not got a petty bone in my body. He hopes Jamie doesn't leave her or break her heart because what would be the point of everything he's gone through just for her to end up with a sore heart like his? It's not as if she'll come back to him now. He entertained that for a while. But no. Too far down the road now. Said too many bad things. She actually said to Malcolm that she preferred men that didn't talk so much. 'I prefer the silent types.' Nee naw nee naw nee naw. She said, 'You don't talk, Malcolm, you rant. On and on and on as only you can go and I'm tired of it, Malcolm, I'm tired of you ranting.' Blaaah di blah di blah. Excuse me? Glasgow is jam-packed with ranting men. Aaaaaaach. A good rant is good for you like a big bowl of porridge. He sometimes feels as if porridge is coming out of his mouth when he is ranting. Splurge. Grey. Lumpy. Thick.

At least he admits his bad points. Give him his due.

He is messy. He is prone to a bit of ranting here and there. He has a temper. He is prone to depression. He doesn't get round to doing things as quickly as he should these days. What does the ex-wife admit to? Bugger all. She's got no faults whatsoever by the way, she's perfect. She was perfect, you know. He wishes he'd seen that at the time. He wishes he'd seen that when she lay in bed next to him for fifteen years. She said to him a month or so ago, 'It's been a long time, Malcolm, move on. You're a long time dead. Get yourself a new girlfriend.' But he is not interested, has absolutely not a bit of interest in lumbering himself with a new girlfriend. The only thing he is interested in is in killing himself. That's the one thing he finds exciting. That's the big thrill in his life at the moment. In any case, he's not certain he'd manage that whole business any more. It's all right for women; they can fake it but for a man it's a little bit obvious, you know. He is frightened. He is more frightened of never getting a hard-on ever again than he is of killing himself.

It's three in the morning and Malcolm is just lying here not achieving very much. He lights up a smoke and stares at the ceiling. He is so crap he can't even come up with a decent plan without veering off his subject. He can't seem to stick his mind to anything these days. He used to be able to when he was working. He used to be Mr Malcolm efficient Jobson – 'Ask

Malcolm to do something and he will do it.' He may as
well get up. He doesn't need to get dressed because he
is dressed already. What's the point in taking clothes off
when you've only to put them back on again? When the
drink wears off, he wakes up. He gets maybe three to
four hours' sleep. Maybe you can't even call that sleep.
Three hours unconscious and then bang! The eyes
open, the thoughts buzz, round and round and round
and round in his head. There's nothing new to think.
It's just the same stuff that goes round and comes back
like a bad digestive system. Like a bat circling the same
patch of sky. Malcolm keeps trying to work it out.
When exactly she started with him. How she started
with him. When, how. How, when. He imagines Jamie
will be a bit of a Casanova in the bedroom, not that
Malcolm was a wham bam thank you ma'am, but still.
Aaaaach. Dirty – dirty – dirty.

He goes into his bathroom and takes a leak. It's a
long alcoholic leak, bright jaundiced yellow. It goes on
for ages and is very noisy. He's a bit jangled. That
Schubert is playing again, the Unfinished one they
played the other day, playing in his head without the
radio on. His kidneys are a bit tender like his balls, his
wee disappointed balls. It's cold. This house is cold.
There's boxes of his stuff not unpacked yet so that
should make things easier for them when they're clear-
ing it all away. He got a letter the other day, can't

remember when because the days have got mixed up. It said – wait a minute, here it is in his trouser pocket. Actually, let him have a fag to go with it – 'Dear Malcolm, the kids are missing you and I want everything to be better between us. Would you like to come for your tea? Jamie is fine about you coming for tea and will be here too. For the sake of the kids, let's try a bit harder. Let's forget the past. I promise not to mention the computer again. I don't want to deny our kids their dad. With love, Katie.' He could tell from the wording of that letter that it was not hers, it was his, pretending to be hers. She never, ever wrote *with love*. He didn't even think she'd know that you could do that, write *with love*; she'd know about *warm wishes* and *all the best* if she wanted to be a bit frosty, and *lots of love* if she wanted to be very warm, and plain *love* if she wanted to be non-committal, but not *with love*. She used to write *love* on every single note – even the ones she left about the house asking for him to get more milk. She was a contradiction like that, you know. The things she wrote down were warmer than her in person. That sounds like she's dead, Malcolm thought. Well, in a way, she is, you know, in a way she is dead.

He washes his face with cold water. He brushes his teeth. The toothpaste has run out so he does his best with his brush and tries and makes a mental note. Get some toothpaste, Malkie, because even if you die very soon, you want to die with fresh breath. Ditto being clean. He takes his clothes off and jumps in the shower. He washes his body. He washes his legs and in between his toes and behind his ears and behind his neck like his mother taught him. The soap is wearing thin and slithering out of his hand onto the floor. He can see through it. He gets out of the shower and dries himself with a damp towel. Katie was right – you should hang the fucking towels up or else when you come to use them again they're damp and you're full of regret. He tries to find a pair of clean boxers. This is a bit of a challenge by the way and he can't remember when he last did a big wash. He looks inside his machine and there's a whole wash in there damp as well and smelling the way a wash does when it's not taken out and hung up, like smelly socks or something bad you ate that comes back to you. Christ, Malkie, he says to himself, if you're going to kill yourself, you're going to have to get a bit more organized.

He doesn't like the idea of being dead and Katie coming round here to clear away his things and seeing the state of the place. That would be a dead giveaway as well. It's half-past three in the fucking morning and he's hoovering his place, standing starkers in his bollocks because he can't find clean boxer shorts and he's put some on the radiator to dry. It's freezing and he feels a bit pervy being naked and hoovering until he has a brainwave. He rushes back to his bedroom and hunts through his drawers. He pulls everything out, jumpers, T-shirts, sweatshirts, God he needs to sort all this out, this is out of order, till finally he finds them. He puts on his old swimming trunks, that's better. He taught all his bairns to swim, by the way: breast stroke, crawl, even butterfly. People doing the butterfly look mental, don't they. What a contortion the butterfly is.

He can't remember when he last got the fucking hoover out either. It's like the months since they split have passed in a fug. The fucking thing isn't picking up properly. Bastard fucking hoover! He takes the bag out and empties it in the kitchen bin and half of it goes in the bin and the other half of it falls on the floor. Grey munchy dust; maybe that's what heaven looks like. Maybe heaven isn't white at all but more like clouds of hoover dust. Who knows? He'll not be finding out because even if he manages to hide his suicide from all his living relatives, he won't be hiding it from God supposing there is a God. He must admit you start to have your wee doubts when you're involved in a big plan like this. Put it this way, you are more likely to say you're an agnostic than an out-and-out atheist at this stage in the game.

He attaches the hoover bag into the hoover again which takes ages because his hands are trembling. Stupid things. Trembling like fucking Mohammed Ali's hands in the end, you know. Big Cassius Clay, what a man, eh? He remembers years ago before they had a telly, when he was a boy, standing outside a telly shop in Argyll Street with about a hundred other people crammed and jammed against the window watching the big match between him and Foreman out in the street.

He turns the hoover on again. The dog runs out of the room. It's only when the dog does that and he sees the wary look in the dog's eye that he thinks to himself: Christ, the dog. He'd forgotten all about the dog even though he'd been feeding it. He'd not considered the dog's role in his private life, in his topping himself. The dog is a bit of a problem, really. Another thing he is going to have to chew over. That Jamie doesn't like dogs is the only reason he has got the dog. His kids will miss their dog and he doesn't want to kill the dog too. What's she done? Actually she's the only one that's really been his pal during all this autumn through to winter. The amount of times that dog has looked into his eyes; he swears she knows his secret. She gives him this despondent, self-pitying look that is quite something to behold.

No matter. He'll consider that later. Polo would be happier with the kids anyway. Polo misses the kids and the wife. And if he were actually gone, then Jamie would have to be persuaded. Polo has had a hang-dog expression ever since the house was sold and they came to live in this wee place in the Milton. The wife is living in the Briggs. At first they thought that would be easier for them, not that far between them. They might be just a few miles down the road from each other, but Malcolm actually feels like they are living in different universes. He doesn't recognize her, do you know. Maybe it's me, maybe it's all me, he thinks to himself. He first knew that he was depressed when he lost interest in football. He'd been a big Celtic fan all his life since the days of Kenny Dalglish, the first. Suddenly there he was one day a couple of years ago, big match on the telly and he turned it over. Years of him saying wheeesht to his kids when the football was on only to have no kids and no football now. No telly, actually. When he was working he had a season ticket and went all over the fucking place with the football. He was in Barcelona once and he said to his pals, 'Look at the bloody Spanish, aren't they good-looking?' He wasn't even commenting on the women; it was the men, actually. Good-looking big bastards. He said to his pals, 'We Scottish must be the ugliest bunch of bastards in the world.' And one of his pals says, 'Speak fir yoursell.'

If he went out with the dog, drove over the Campsie Glens into the Fintry Hills and just set off on those rough-looking moors when the temperature is below freezing with a bottle of Bell's, the dog would probably

get found by somebody. That was one possibility. Drink
the bottle and lie down in the cold in such a way that
looks like he's fallen over. And freeze to fucking death.
No but he doesn't fancy that much, though. Too chilly.
What else. C'mon, Malkie, think. Use the loaf. Use the
head. All the usual paths for the blue people are closed
to him. He can't take pills. There has to be a way.

It's four thirty now and it's still very dark outside.
Very wintry dark. He goes right outside and looks up at
the stars. Every constellation you could name or imagine is up there tonight; the stars have a ball when it's
freezing cold. He was teaching Jojo about the stars a
few months back, well those he knows anyway. The
Plough, the Bear, the brightest planet. Jojo got up
because Jojo heard them fighting and he took him out
for a wee minute to look at the stars and Katie comes
out and says, 'Are you out of your mind, he'll catch his
death.' He goes back inside the house that doesn't feel
like his and opens the curtains properly. Quiet out there
in the Milton. Hardly any lights on. One or two, probably old insomniacs, mucking about in their kitchens,
getting a cup of tea or talking to their cat. Not a huge
amount goes on at this hour during the week anyway.
He goes to light a cigarette and thinks to himself that
he may as well give up smoking. It's one thing he could
actually achieve before he dies. He could say to himself,
Well at least before you died you gave up smoking.

The same goes for drinking when he thinks about it. Today on his last day he is not under any circumstances whatsoever going to drink and he is not going to smoke which rules out the Fintry whisky option. Even supposing it takes him another three weeks to pull it off, a fag will not cross his lips or a wee nip of anything, no Bell's, no Teacher's, no special malts. Absolutely, unequivocally nothing. Not a nippy nothing. In the middle of the night, with his swimming trunks on and the hoovering finished, Malcolm Henry Jobson makes up his mind to straighten himself up before he takes himself out.

Weddings and Beheadings
Hanif Kureishi

I have gathered the equipment together and now I am waiting for them to arrive. They will not be long; they never are.

You don't know me personally. My existence has never crossed your mind. But I would bet you've seen my work: it has been broadcast everywhere, on most of the news channels worldwide. Or at least parts of it have. You could find it on the Internet, right now, if you really wanted to. If you could bear to look.

Not that you'd notice my style, my artistic signature or anything like that. I film beheadings, which are common in this war-broken city, my childhood home.

It was never my ambition, as a young man who loved cinema, to film such things. Nor was it my wish to do weddings either, though there are less of those these days. Ditto graduations and parties. My friends and I have always wanted to make real films, with living actors and dialogue and jokes and music, as we began to do as students. Nothing like that is possible any more. Every day we are ageing, we feel shabby. The stories are there, waiting to be told; we're artists. But this stuff, the death work, it has taken over.

We were 'recommended' for this employment, and we can't not do it; we can't say we're visiting relatives or working in the cutting room. They call us up with little notice at odd hours, usually at night, and minutes later they are outside with their guns. They put us in the car and cover our heads. Because there's only one of us working at a time, the thugs help with carrying the gear. But we have to do the sound as well as the picture, and load the camera and work out how to light the scene. I've asked to use an assistant yet they only offer their rough accomplices who know nothing, who can't even wipe a lens without making a mess of it.

I know three other guys who do this work; we discuss it amongst ourselves, but we'd never talk to anyone else or we'd end up in front of the camera.

Until recently my closest friend filmed beheadings; however, he's not a director, only a writer really. I wouldn't say anything, but I wouldn't trust him with a camera. He isn't too sure about the technical stuff, how to set up the equipment, and then how to get the material through the computer and onto the Internet. It's a skill, obviously.

He was the one who had the idea of getting calling cards with 'Weddings and Beheadings' inscribed on them. If the power's on, we meet in his flat to watch movies on video. When we part he jokes, 'Don't bury your head in the sand, my friend. Don't go losing your head now. Chin up!'

A couple of weeks ago he messed up badly. The cameras are good quality, they're taken from foreign journalists, but a bulb blew in the one light he was using, and he couldn't replace it. By then they had brought the victim in. My friend tried to tell the men, 'It's too dark, it's not going to come out and you can't do another take.' But they were in a hurry, he couldn't persuade them to wait, they were already hacking through the neck and he was in such a panic he fainted. Luckily the camera was running. It came out underlit of course – what did they expect? I liked it; Lynchian, I called it, but they hit him around the head, and never used him again.

He was lucky. But I wonder if he's going mad. Secretly he kept copies of his beheadings and now he plays around with them on his computer, cutting and re-cutting them, putting them to music, swing stuff, opera, jazz, comic songs. Perhaps it's the only freedom he has.

It might surprise you, but we do get paid; they always give us something 'for the trouble'. They even make jokes, 'You'll get a prize for the next one. Don't you guys love prizes and statuettes and stuff?'

It's all hellish, the long drive there with the camera and tripod on your lap, the smell of the sack, the guns, and you wonder if this time you might be the victim. Usually you're sick, and then you're in the building, in the room, setting up, and you hear things, from other rooms, that make you wonder if life on earth is a good idea.

I know you don't want too much detail, but it's serious work taking off someone's head if you're not a butcher; and these guys aren't qualified, they're just enthusiastic – it's what they like to do. To make the shot work, it helps to get a clear view of the victim's eyes just before they're covered. At the end the guys hold up the head streaming with blood and you might need to use some hand-held here, to catch everything. The shot must be framed carefully. It wouldn't be good if you missed something. [Ideally you should have a quick-release tripod head, something I do possess and would never lend to anyone.]

They cheer and fire off rounds while you're checking the tape and playing it back. Afterwards, they put the body in a bag and dump it somewhere, before they drive you to another place, where you transfer the material to the computer and send it out.

Often I wonder what this is doing to me. I think of

war photographers, who, they say, use the lens to distance themselves from the reality of suffering and death. But those guys have elected to do that work, they believe in it. We are innocent.

One day I'd like to make a proper film, maybe beginning with a beheading, telling the story that leads up to it. It's the living I'm interested in, but the way things are going I'll be doing this for a while. Sometimes I wonder if I'm going to go mad, or whether even this escape is denied me.

I better go now. Someone is at the door.

Biographical Notes

DAVID ALMOND grew up in a large Catholic family on Tyneside. His short story collections include *Counting Stars* and *A Kind of Heaven*. During the early 90s, he edited the fiction magazine *Panurge*.

His first novel for children, *Skellig*, won the Carnegie Medal, the Whitbread Award, and became a bestseller around the world. The novels, plays and stories that followed have brought popular success, widespread critical acclaim, and a string of major prizes, including the Michael L. Printz Award (USA) and a second Whitbread Award. His work has been translated into over twenty languages, and adapted for film, radio and stage. His most recent novel is *Clay*.

Forthcoming are two short novels, *My Dad's a Birdman* and *The Savage*; a stage version of *The Fire-Eaters*; and an opera of *Skellig*.

He lives with his family in Northumberland. His website is at www.davidalmond.com.

JONATHAN FALLA was born in Jamaica, won a scholarship to Cambridge and a Fulbright Fellowship to USC in Los Angeles. A nurse, he worked for aid agencies in Indonesia, Uganda, Burma, Nepal and Sudan, experiences which provided material for a theatre comedy about famine relief and a novel, *Poor Mercy*, set in Darfur. His first novel, *Blue Poppies*, described the Chinese invasion of Tibet. He has also written a BBC film, *The Hummingbird Tree*; a study of rebel tribes in Burma, *True Love & Bartholomew*; a musical for children, *River of Dreams*, and numerous stories and essays.

A lutenist and singer, he works with an Early Music quartet performing Renaissance chamber music. This has led to a new novel based on the lives of Michel de Montaigne and Samuel Scheidt, for which he recently received a Creative Scotland Award. He is currently a Royal Literary Fund Fellow at Dundee University.

JULIAN GOUGH was born in London, to parents so Irish they both have the right to be buried on the Rock of Cashel. When he was seven, the family returned to Tipperary. He was educated by the Christian Brothers, back in the days when they were still allowed to throw a boy across the room. At university in Galway, he began writing and singing with the underground rock band, Toasted Heretic, which had a top ten hit in

Ireland in 1991 with 'Galway and Los Angeles', a song about not kissing Sinead O'Connor.

His first novel, *Juno & Juliet*, was published in 2001. His second novel, *Jude: Level 1*, will be published in July 2007 by Old Street Publishing. Gough believes (as did the Greeks at the time of Aristophanes) that tragedy is merely the human view of life: comedy is superior, being the gods' view.

The self-contained story 'The Orphan and the Mob' also forms the prologue to *Jude: Level 1*. Julian says: 'It's like the bit at the start of the *Star Wars* trilogy, where Luke Skywalker is working on his uncle's farm, and then the planet's destroyed, and he has to go off on his galactic quest and discover his destiny. Except set in Tipperary.' His website and blog, at www.julian gough.com, explores more of the cultural space between Aristophanes and *Star Wars*.

JACKIE KAY was born in Edinburgh in 1961 and grew up in Glasgow. She has published four collections of poetry, the first of which, *The Adoption Papers* (1991), won the Saltire and Forward Prizes. The second, *Other Lovers* (1993), won the Somerset Maugham Award.

Jackie Kay's first novel, *Trumpet*, won the *Guardian* Fiction Prize and the Authors' Club First Novel Award. Her first collection of short stories, *Why Don't You Stop Talking*, was published by Picador in 2002 and her second, *Wish I Was Here*, in 2006. She has also written books for children, and a monograph on Bessie Smith.

Jackie Kay lives in Manchester with her son.

HANIF KUREISHI was born and brought up in Kent. He read Philosophy at King's College London, where he started to write plays. In 1981 he won the George Devine Award for his play *Outskirts*, and in 1982 he was appointed Writer in Residence at the Royal Court Theatre. In 1984 he wrote the screenplay *My Beautiful Laundrette*, which was made into a film by Stephen Frears and for which Kureishi received an Oscar nomination. Two more films followed: *Sammy and Rosie Get Laid* and *London Kills Me*, which he also directed.

His first novel, *The Buddha of Suburbia* (1990) won the Whitbread First Novel Award and was televised by the BBC. This was followed by *The Black Album* (1995), *Intimacy* (1998) and two collections of short stories, *Love in a Blue Time* (1997) and *Midnight All Day* (1999). The story 'My Son the Fanatic', from *Love in a Blue Time*, was made into a film in 1998, and in 1999 a new play, *Sleep With Me*, was staged at the National Theatre.

Gabriel's Gift, Kureishi's fourth novel, was published in 2001. A collection of essays, *Dreaming and Scheming*, and a volume of short stories, *The Body*, were published in 2002. A film of his screenplay, *The Mother*, directed by Robert Mitchell, was released in 2003. *My Ear at His*

Heart, a memoir about his father, was published in 2004, and a book of essays, *The Word and the Bomb,* was published in 2005. A film of his latest screenplay, *Venus,* was released in the UK in January 2007. He has been awarded the Chevalier de l'Ordre des Arts des Lettres.

Hanif Kureishi lives in West London.